D1650796

TORN BETWEEN A GOON AND A GANGSTA 2

A NOVEL BY

JADE JONES

www.jadedpublications.com

To be notified of new releases, contests, giveaways, and book signings in your area, text **BOOKS** to **25827**

This novel is a work of fiction. Any reference to real people, events, establishments, or locales is intended only to give the fiction a sense of reality and authenticity. Other names, characters, and incidents occurring in the work are either the product of the author's imagination or are used fictitiously, as are those fictionalized events and events that involve real persons. Any character that happens to share the name of a person who is any acquaintance of the author, past or present, is purely coincidental and is in no way intended to be an actual account involving that person.

Copyright © 2013

All rights reserved, including the right to reproduce this book or portion thereof in any form whatsoever

Acknowledgments

First, I would like to thank the Lord for blessing me with the gift of creativity and also helping me to perfect it. Of course, I can't forget about my own group, Jaded Publications Fan Group. Thank you so much for all the love and support. To all my readers and supporters, thank you.

1

"Damn, I can't believe we did that shit, bro!" Hassan said excitedly.

The rush from getting away with what he had just done felt so great. Much like a welcome relief or a breath of fresh air. The shit he had pulled was a long time coming; a betrayal brewing for many months.

Hassan then peered out the window in order to see if anyone was pursuing them. It seemed silly, but he didn't like the fact that Nikki had gotten away.

I should have put a bullet in that bitch before I shot Dre, he told himself. Oh well. He figured she wouldn't be able to survive on her own anyway. With the Feds looking for her, and her face plastered all over most wanted posters it was pretty much a wrap for her. It was a shame too because Hassan really did have such high hopes for them, and the relationship that could have been.

In a friendship where he always seemed to be the third wheel, Hassan felt good coming out on top. He used Dre and Nikki to lead him right to the money…and they did…

Hassan relaxed in his seat after he realized they weren't being pursued. "Damn," he said. "We did it, bro."

Careem eased the car to a stop at a red traffic light. "Yeah...we did it...," he said before suddenly putting the barrel of his gun to Hassan's temple.

Hassan sighed in disappointment after realizing what was going on. He couldn't believe that his own brother had set him up simply because he did not want to divide the money.

All this time Hassan thought he was the one who had been schemin' when his brother, Careem was the one who had been plotting against him all along.

Ain't this about a fucking bitch, Hassan asked himself.

He wondered if Careem really had it in him to pull the trigger...

"Damn, bro," Hassan said. "So this is what this shit all comes down to? You just gon' shoot a nigga, huh?" he asked.

Careem offered a devilish smile and shrugged. "Nothin' personal," he said before cocking the Glock.

In a sudden, swift movement, Hassan knocked away the gun milliseconds before Careem was able to put a bullet in his little brother's head.

POP!

The gun instantly went off! A bullet whizzed past Hassan's head, slightly grazing his left ear.

Careem and Hassan wrestled with each other for possession of the gun. The battle was indeed one of life and death and both brothers were determined to come out the victor. It was fucked up how quick money could change a person.

Blood seeped from the small cut on the rim of Hassan's ear. It then trailed down the side of his neck.

Spittle flew from Careem's mouth as he bared his teeth like a madman. Mustering up all his strength, he tried to regain possession of the gun. The traffic light had turned green seconds earlier, but Careem's sports car sat stationed several feet from the light. There wasn't another car or person in sight to witness the battle between both brothers.

Hassan's hands were wrapped tightly around the barrel of the gun. Careem's hands were gripped firmly around the butt. Hoarse groans and deep, guttural grunts were the only sounds perceivable. The gun slowly aimed towards the sky.

POP!

The gun went off a second time. Nearby birds scattered in the distance. Hassan quickly gained the upper hand as he turned the barrel of the gun towards Careem.

POP!

Careem's index finger accidentally squeezed the trigger causing the gun to go off a third time. A bullet quickly lodged deep into Careem's shoulder just beneath his collarbone.

"*Aarrrgghh*!" he cried out in agony. Careem released his grip from the gun in order to cradle his injured shoulder. Pain shot throughout his entire body.

Hassan quickly aimed the barrel of the gun in Careem's direction. "Get the fuck out of the car!" he spat.

Blood quickly spurted from Careem's wound as he stared at Hassan in disbelief. He was expecting a bullet to his dome at any minute.

"You heard me nigga! Get out the mothafuckin' car!" Hassan yelled.

He wasn't fucking around and his tone hinted just that. Right about now, Careem was not his brother in his eyes. He was simply a money hungry, selfish, greedy mothafucka whom had just betrayed his own flesh and blood. To put it simple, he was an enemy; and Hassan knew just how to deal with enemies and people of the like...

Careem's nostrils flared wildly as he stared into his brother's cold eyes. Hesitantly, he opened the driver door and stumbled out of the car. Hassan quickly did the same, making sure to keep his gaze locked intensely on Careem.

Careem continued to hold onto his injured shoulder, keeping his palm pressed flatly against the bullet wound. However that did little next to nothing to ease the bleeding.

"So you gon' shoot me mothafucka?!" Careem yelled.

Without uttering a word, Hassan quickly rounded the car and kept the gun aimed at Careem.

"Huh?!" Careem spat. "*You gon' shoot me mothafucka*?!" he repeated.

Hassan quickly approached his brother. Without warning, he smacked the butt of the gun directly against Careem's skull.

Careem dropped onto the pavement instantaneously after the unexpected blow.

"You were gonna kill *me*, nigga!" Hassan shouted. "Yo' own mothafuckin' brother! Yo' flesh and blood!" he yelled. "Over some mothafuckin' money? Are you serious, my nigga?!" Hassan was pumped up from the entire ordeal as he paced back and forth.

Careem stared up at Hassan from the ground. A tiny glint of fear flashed in his eyes. Unfortunately, he didn't think about the possibility of the tables being turned against him. He figured he had it all planned out. He'd kill Hassan and effortlessly make off with money. Never did he think he'd be the one staring down the barrel of a gun.

Suddenly, Careem's life flashed before his eyes. Instead of thinking about his child or current girlfriend, he was thinking that he had not made entirely enough money in his lifetime.

Ain't this a mothafucka, he asked himself. He actually considered begging Hassan for his life, but the pride in him wouldn't allow him to go out like a bitch.

"Nigga, fuck you!" Careem spat.

Hassan instantly looked offended. "Oh…fuck *me*?" he asked in disbelief. "Fuck *me*?" He stepped closer to Careem and aimed the gun at his own brother. "Nah mothafucka. Fuck you!" Hassan said through gritted teeth.

Careem slowly scooted away from Hassan. The soles on his Jordans scraped against the pavement as he backed up. Deep down inside, he was scared shitless to die, but he chose to front like he wasn't.

"You ain't gon' kill me, nigga. Why you flexin'?" he asked looking up at Hassan.

Hassan's nostrils flared wildly as he stared into Careem's dark eyes. His index finger squeezed gently on the trigger. He was fighting his own demons. Pulling the trigger on his longtime friends proved to be easier than shooting his own flesh and blood.

Careem immediately took note of Hassan's hesitancy and resorted to provoking him. "Yeah, just like I thought," he taunted. "You can't even pull the fuckin' trigger! You's a lil' bitch wit' yo' soft, punk ass! Always have been a lil' bitch! And you wonder why that hoe ain't want yo weak ass!" he said to referring to Nikki.

That insult actually hit a nerve. Hassan's jaw muscle tightened as he stared at his brother lying pathetically on the street. He squinted his eyes and licked his lips. *Just shoot this mothafucka and bounce,* he told himself. He would deal with his conscience later.

Careem suddenly broke into a fit of sadistic laughter. "You might as well drop that gun, boy," he taunted. "You ain't gon' do shit anyway! You heard me, mothafucka!" Careem screamed. "You ain't gon' do—"

POP!

A single bullet struck Careem directly in the face.

***

Nikki's back was pressed firmly against the brick wall of a building. Standing alone in an empty alley, on the run from the law, she had no idea what her fate would entail. Her grip around her pistol was firm.

Nikki slowly looked up. Thin wispy clouds were scattered across the bright sky. She then closed her eyes and inhaled deeply. Her heart thumped rapidly in her chest. She could clearly hear it beating loudly in her head. Sadly, it beat for Dre.

She had witnessed Hassan damn near empty an entire clip into Dre's body. Hassan had murdered the love of her life without so much as a second thought or hint of regret...and then to make matters worse, he had unexpectedly turned the gun on her.

"Lord...if you can hear me...," Nikki whispered. "Please...please let me make it out of this alive," she prayed. "Let me make it out of this alive so I can kill that backstabbing, piece of—

Urrgghhhnnn! *Urrgghhhnnn*!

The sudden wail of nearby ambulance and police car sirens drowned out Nikki's words. Evidently, they were headed to the Baxter home. With all the noise and gunshots they were bound to come eventually.

Nikki tucked her pistol inside her jumpsuit, and waited patiently until the sound of sirens faded before she finally left the alley. Wearing a navy electrician jumpsuit, she prayed she wouldn't be recognized. She looked over her shoulder every few steps she took out of sheer paranoia. Ten minutes from downtown Cleveland, Nikki had quite a nice long walk on her hands.

Tears slipped from both her eyes, but she quickly wiped them away before they were able to roll of her chin. The realization of Dre's death was still dawning on her. His murder had taken place no less than an hour ago. The shit felt so unrealistic. She couldn't believe that Hassan had actually turned on them.

She knew that he was upset she had chosen Dre over him, but she had no idea that he would resort to that level of betrayal. Hassan didn't give a damn about trying to kill Nikki. A woman that was possibly carrying his child. If that wasn't fucked up, Nikki did not know what was.

The minute Hassan and Nikki crossed paths again, she vowed to herself that she'd put a bullet right in between his light brown eyes.

***

Gold all in my chain.

Gold all in my ring.

Gold all in my watch.

Don't believe just watch.

Maceo nodded his head to the beat of Trinidad James' "*All Gold Everything*" as he cruised up the street in his gun metal black and silver trim Chrysler 300 which sat on twenty-six inch chrome rims.

His ten karat diamond pavé bracelet glimmered on his right wrist as he steered. A gold chain hung loosely around his neck. Full sleeve tattoos adorned both his toned arms from his wrists to his shoulders. His full beard was trimmed neatly and his bald head was shined to perfection. Maceo was sexy as hell in a rugged, mannish sort of way.

The money from selling guns and weaponry paid his bills. It also brought his jewelry, his custom Chrysler 300 and his Harley-Davidson V-Rod. The consequences and stakes were also high for orchestrating such an illegal hustle. Maceo had already served two years in a federal prison on gun charges after he was pulled over by a state trooper. The moment, the cop popped the trunk Maceo already knew it was a wrap.

Maceo served his time, but didn't allow the sentence to deter him in the least. He still did what he did best. After all, it was the only hustle he knew, and he was damn sure good at it.

Maceo had just come from getting his iPhone fixed at the repair shop on West 25th. He loved the popular cell phone but he'd be damned if he wasn't at the repair shop every other week for some sort of issue with his phone. This time it was for an air bubble beneath the screen. Last week he was having Wi-Fi issues. He was damn near ready to sell the piece of shit and go cop a cheap Boost Mobile flip phone.

Maceo lightly pressed down on the brakes as he approached a yellow traffic light. Suddenly something caught Maceo's attention from the corner of his eye. Walking up the street wearing a navy jumpsuit was a woman who appeared eerily familiar. It was something about her stride. He watched the woman glance over her shoulder several times.

Suddenly it dawned on him where he knew her from. "Damn," Maceo muttered. "What the hell is she doing out here?" He slowly eased his car alongside Nikki and lowered the volume to the CD player.

Nikki quickly took notice of the car pulling beside her. For a moment she feared it might be a squad car, but she was relieved to see that it wasn't. Her heart rate slowed down for a second, and she watched as the passenger window lowered.

"Nikki?" a familiar voice called out to her.

She stopped walking long enough to peer into the vehicle from a safe distance. The silhouette inside looked familiar but she inched closer to the curb just to be sure. After verifying that it was indeed Maceo she walked up to the car.

"Nikki, what the fuck are you doin' walkin' around down here?" Maceo asked.

He couldn't believe that she was walking around like she was not a wanted woman. He saw the news story about the murders and robberies and knew the Feds were looking for her or even information regarding her whereabouts.

"Maceo," Nikki said breathlessly. "I'm in a lot of shit," she admitted.

His eyes then wandered towards her injured arm. "Fuck! You're bleedin'!" he blurted out.

2

Nikki slowly looked down at her wound. The bleeding had long since ceased but with her sleeve partially drenched in dark red blood, one would've thought different.

"I just got grazed," Nikki said nonchalantly. She was trying to remain strong regardless of the throbbing pain in her arm.

"Damn, you were shot?" Maceo asked in disbelief. "What the hell happened—Get in," he ushered.

Nikki opened the passenger door, and Maceo quickly cleared off the seat before she climbed in. The heat was turned up to its maximum and it instantly soothed her since she'd been walking in forty-degree weather.

"What the fuck is goin' on, ma?" Maceo asked in a concerned tone before pulling off.

Nikki fought from breaking down right then and there. She tried desperately to hold it together. "Can we just get away from here?" she asked. "Please, Maceo...I...I just wanna get far away from here...and then I'll tell you everything." Her voice cracked as she spoke. Her emotions were beginning to overwhelm her. All she could think about was Dre lying in a puddle of his own blood.

"Uh, you want me to take you to the hospital or somethin'?" he asked eyeing her injured arm. "I ain't a doctor, but that shit looks like you really need some medical attention."

"No," Nikki quickly answered. The moment she walked through a hospital's door, she's be apprehended by the security. She would rather risk bleeding out before she blatantly turned herself in.

Maceo turned his attention back to the road and nodded his head in understanding. "My bad, ma," he said in a low tone. "I forgot just that quick...I don't even know why I would suggest that shit...I just...all the blood fucked me up, you know."

Maceo had just saw Dre and Hassan a few days ago. Dre had wanted the hookup on some artificial birth certificates and social security cards, but didn't have the money right then to pay for it. Maceo wondered what had happened in between then and now.

"Aye, where's my boy, Dre?" he asked turning towards Nikki.

Tears quickly filled Nikki's eyes at the mere mention of Dre. She slowly turned her head away and glanced out the window at the passing scenery. Nikki hoped Maceo would take the hint and drop the painful subject. She did not want to talk about the shit that had taken place at Timothy Baxter's home.

***

Blood trailed from the corner of Dre's mouth down the side of his face. With each second that passed, he could slowly feel his life slipping away. The sound of sirens was so close that if he had to guess he would say that the police and ambulance had finally arrived.

Dre prayed that he would die before he was able to be apprehended by the police. If he lived, they'd simply throw his black ass in jail and throw away the key. He would never see Nikki again.

Nikki...

A single tear slipped from the corner of his eye. Dre was sure that Hassan had killed her even though he had blacked out after he hit the floor. He tried to crane his neck to look around the living room for Nikki's body, but couldn't even execute a simple motion.

Never in a million years would he have thought his boy would have turned on him like that.

Suddenly, Dre heard the sound of heavy footsteps storm into the home. He tried to move again but was totally immobilized. Several police officers rushed the scene just as Dre blacked out...

***

Hassan navigated the sports car far away from the fatal scene he had left behind. Rocko's new single "*Nachos*" blared through the custom speakers.

He had left Careem lying outstretched in the middle of the street in a puddle of his own blood.

Hassan had won...but unfortunately he did not feel like a winner. To be honest, he felt like a damn loser. He felt like shit when he should have been feeling like he was on top of the world.

Hassan had the money, his life, and his freedom...but that realization meant nothing since he no longer had anyone to share the victory with. Less than an hour after shooting Dre, his conscience was already eating away at his sanity. He had been so heartless when he pulled the trigger on Dre, the Baxter family, Careem, and Nikki...why was he suddenly feeling sorry about it now?

Hassan sighed dejectedly.

Nikki.

His heart instantly dropped into the pit of his stomach. She was still alive. Alive and out there somewhere possibly carrying his child. He figured a bullet to her dome would erase any and all feelings he had for her. He'd be free of the spell she had unintentionally casted upon him. Unfortunately, things did not go as planned. Nikki had somehow evaded death. And knowing her, she was probably ready and willing to seek revenge. She was just that type of woman.

BEEP!

Hassan quickly slammed his foot onto the brakes. The firestone tires burned the asphalt as he forced the car to a sudden stop. He had accidentally run a red light and nearly collided with a furniture moving truck. The sports car skirted to a stop seconds before colliding with the large truck.

The driver of the moving truck honked his horn in irritation. Hassan had to be blind to not notice the traffic crossing at the busy intersection. Instead of paying attention his mind was focused on everything that had taken place in less than an hour's span.

Hassan punched the center of the steering wheel in a sudden fit of rage. "*Damn*!" he yelled.

BEEP!

The horn blared after the impact. The traffic behind him was just beginning to move again. Drivers couldn't resist the temptation to peer into Hassan's car at him as they drove around his vehicle.

"I'm too fuckin' tense," he told himself. "I need to chill out and relax." He needed to smoke.

Hassan hated to admit it, but he was a tad bit fucked up emotionally after all the blood he had shed today. He needed time to sit, think, and organize his thoughts. He needed to clear his mind before he went crazy. Fortunately, he knew of a perfect way to release his frustrations.

Twenty minutes later, Hassan pulled into the driveway of a quaint yellow home located off Clark Avenue on the west side of Cleveland. After parking the car, Hassan popped the trunk. Grabbing the duffel bag full of money and jewelry, he climbed out and rounded the car. He then tossed the duffel bag into the trunk and slammed it close. The moment he looked up, he noticed Fiona standing on the porch hugging herself in an attempt to keep warm from the cool breeze.

She wore a pair of striped pajama pants and a light blue thermal. A scarf was wrapped around her hair, and it was apparent that she was not expecting company.

Hassan had been fucking with Fiona ever since their little rendezvous at the nightclub where they had met. He kept her around simply for intimate purposes only.

"I wish you would have told me that you were coming over," she said. "You could have at least called...What if I had company—"

"Then tell that mothafucka he gotta bounce," Hassan said making his way towards the house.

Fiona looked offended, but she didn't respond.

"What?" Hassan asked. "You gotta nigga in here?" He skipped up the steps and boldly invited himself into Fiona's home.

"No, I don't," Fiona said stepping back inside behind Hassan.

Hassan quickly took in his surroundings. Indeed Fiona was alone.

Fiona folded her arms underneath her large, perky breasts. "What's up with you Mr. Attitude?" she asked sarcastically. Fiona wasn't used to seeing this side of Hassan. She wondered what the hell was wrong with him.

Hassan slowly turned around and faced Fiona. Even in her PJs she looked sexy as hell. She reminded him of a brown skinned version of Lauren London. She had a micro dermal diamond piercing beside her left eye. "My bad," he apologized. "I just...I'm having a fucked up day," he sighed.

Fiona padded over towards Hassan. "Poor baby," she purred in a seductive tone. "You wanna tell me about it?" She moved in to kiss his lips but he evaded it by leaning down to kiss her neck instead.

Kissing was far too intimate. Hassan only shared that level of intimacy with Nikki...and unfortunately it led to his feelings being hurt. He made a vow to himself that he'd never let a woman as close to his heart as Nikki was. His father had told him about women as a young boy and now he was receiving a crash course.

Hassan wrapped his hands around Fiona's tiny waist. Just holding her close had his dick hard. He reminisced about the way she rode his dick in the VIP room of the nightclub. Every time they got together she always managed to put it on him and that's why he couldn't get enough of her now.

A soft moan escaped through Fiona's full lips as Hassan kissed the silky flesh of her throat softly. His dick strained against the fabric of his denim jeans. Not wanting to waste any more time, he eased Fiona's pajama pants down her legs and assisted her with stepping out of the pants legs. The moment his face was level with her waist, he eyed her shaven kitty.

Hassan wet his lips and looked up at Fiona. Smirking slightly, he asked, "You did that for me?"

Fiona offered a girlish smile. "Yeah," she answered.

Hassan knew she was most likely lying but it didn't even matter. Right about now, he just wanted to bury himself deep into something warm and wet.

Hassan stood to his feet and took Fiona by the hand. "Come here," he whispered leading her towards the living room.

The thirty-two inch flat panel television was turned to one of the Music Choice channels. Gucci Mane and Trey Songz "Beat It Up" was playing. The song fit the mood perfectly, almost as if on cue.

Hassan slowly leaned Fiona over the arm of her nude Jordan sofa. He gave her round, plump ass a firm slap before he proceeded to unbutton his Levis. After stepping out of his jeans, he pulled his rock hard dick through the opening of his boxers and slid a Magnum down his lengthy shaft.

Fiona tooted up her ass up seductively, welcoming Hassan to invade her threshold. He took hold of her curvy hips and slid inside her drenched pussy.

"Oooohhh, shit," Fiona whimpered upon his entrance.

Hassan firmly gripped her waist, pulling her into his strong humps. The sound of skin slapping reverberated off the thin walls of Fiona's small living room.

"Damn, Hassan, Fiona cried. "Not so hard, baby..."

Hassan ignored her pleas to ease up and instead grabbed a fistful of the back of her shirt. His pelvis slammed harshly against Fiona's backside. Her breasts bounced and swung back and forth underneath the thermal she wore with each powerful stroke that Hassan inflicted.

"Now you gon' act like you can't take this dick," Hassan said breathlessly. "Quit playin' Fiona," he told her.

"Turn me over," she insisted.

Hassan didn't mind simply because he was growing irritated with her running from the dick. He quickly pulled her up and turned her around. She leaned backwards, resting her back against the arm of the sofa. Hassan lifted her left leg over his shoulder and slid deep inside her. The sound of wetness between her thighs was music to his ears.

"Oh, shit! *Fuck me Hassan*!" Fiona cried out.

He took hold of one of her breasts and pinched a nipple beneath the thin fabric of her thermal. His pace sped up once he felt himself approaching a powerful orgasm.

"Damn...," Hassan groaned. "I'm about to cum..."

Fiona reached down and began massaging her swollen clit. "If this pussy is good, then cum for it," she told him.

Hassan loved when Fiona talked shit during sex. It was a major turn on. "Here it comes," he whispered. "*Mmm*," he groaned. His dick jerked wildly as his thick nut spurted into the Trojan magnum. "Damn..."

Fiona came shortly after.

After fixing their clothes, Hassan asked, "Do you gotta Mild or a cigarette?" He needed a smoke something terrible.

"I don't smoke those cancer sticks," Fiona told him. "But I might have a Black and Mild in my bedroom. Hold on."

Hassan gave Fiona's ass another slap as she walked off. He then plopped down on her plush sofa. He was just about to prop his feet atop of the cheap wooden coffee table until he heard suspicious sounds coming from outside. He might have been tripping, but it sounded like someone was in the driveway.

Standing to his feet, Hassan walked over towards the living room window and peered through the burgundy horizontal blinds.

The ignition to Hassan's sports car started just as he noticed an unfamiliar guy behind the wheel. His eyes instantly bulged in his sockets at the realization that he was being car jacked!

"*What the fuck*?!" Hassan barked. He quickly broke out running towards the front door nearly tripping on the foyer rug in the process.

The car quickly backed out of the driveway at the same time Hassan swung the front door open. The young Puerto-Rican guy behind the wheel had the nerve to flash a crooked, malicious smile before skirting off.

"Hey! What the fuck are you doing?!" Hassan screamed. He quickly took off running after his car. "Hey! Stop!"

Hassan ran until his lungs burned from lack of oxygen, but unfortunately he was no match against the sports car. Besides, he smoked way too much.

"*Shit*!" Hassan screamed finally giving up. He snatched the skull cap off his head and tossed it to the ground.

Hassan struggled to catch his breath as he watched the taillights of his car disappear in the distance. His money was gone. Just like that...

Hassan's chest heaved up and down, and his breath showed in the cool air. He wanted to cry right about now. This shit was too unrealistic. It wasn't happening!

"*Ain't this a bitch*?!" Hassan screamed at the top of his lungs. "Fuck me!"

"Hassan?" Fiona called out. She jogged towards him with a worrisome look on her pretty face. "What happened?" she asked breathlessly.

Hassan ran a hand though his curly hair and then squeezed a handful. "What the fuck does it look like?!" he yelled. "Some mothafucka just stole my car!"

"I thought you knew," Fiona said. "There's been a series of car thefts in this neighborhood," she informed him. "It's been all over the news."

Hassan wished he would have known that before he came over. Now his money and valuables were gone just because he had decided that he needed some pussy.

"Fuck! Fuck! Fuck!" Hassan cursed. He could hardly catch his breath. His heart thumped rapidly in his chest. He could not believe that someone had just stolen his car. All the shit he had gone through to obtain the money—it was gone!

"Hassan, we'll call the police," Fiona said. "Just calm down—"

Without warning, Hassan charged full speed towards Fiona and snatched her up by her slender neck.

"Calm down?!" he yelled. "Bitch, you don't know what the fuck I just lost! You don't know what the fuck I had to go through!"

Fiona's eyes bulged in their sockets as she struggled to breathe. Hassan was crushing her windpipes. There wasn't a doubt in her mind that he was about to kill her in the broad daylight in the middle of the street.

3

Fiona clawed at Hassan's hands gripped tightly around her neck. The silk scarf wrapped around her hair slipped off, and her hair unraveled. Tears pooled in her eyes as she struggled to gasp for air. High pitch croaking noises came from her mouth and her knees suddenly gave out beneath her.

Seconds before her life slipped away, Hassan finally released his grip. Fiona instantly dropped to the ground coughing, wheezing, and greedily sucking in air.

He looked down at Fiona positioned on her hands and knees gasping for air. To be honest, he didn't trust her as far as he could throw her. Reaching down, he snatched a fistful of her hair, brutally yanking her head back.

"Do you know the mothafucka that just stole my car?!" he demanded to know. "Did you know he was gon' do that shit?"

"No!" Fiona cried. "I swear!" Tears streamed down her cheeks as she reached for her hair. She was scared for her life.

"Bitch, don't lie to me!" Hassan barked.

"I swear on everything I love!" she cried. Watery mucus trickled from her nose "I didn't even know you were coming over. How could I have known your car was gonna get stolen! Hassan, please!" Fiona begged. "Think about it!"

Fiona had definitely made a valid point. Hesitantly, he released her hair. Fiona crawled into a fetal position on the ground and began sobbing like a newborn baby.

Hassan didn't bother apologizing for his actions. He had more important things to worry about, like how and if he would ever get his damn money back. Pacing back and forth in the middle of the street like a madman he continued to curse about the unfortunate turn of events that had just taken place.

***

Nikki sat in a velvet Parson dining chair, gritting her teeth as she allowed Maceo's younger cousin to stitch up the wound on her arm. Maceo's cousin, Rafael was silently cursing to himself and hoping that blood would not get on the expensive chair. Rafael was a medical student living with his mother, but he had one foot in the door and one foot out. His mother would flip if she came home from work and saw all of this happening in her precious dining room.

Nikki encased her bottom lip with her teeth, but fought to hold back tears. Maceo had told her several times to just look away, but she figured if she just watched and saw the process it would be a lot less painful. Silly reasoning but looking wasn't helping ease up the pain.

Maceo silently admired Nikki's bravery and will to remain strong even though he could tell she was on the verge of tears.

Nikki slowly looked up and noticed Maceo staring at her. He looked back down at her arm avoiding her gaze. The last thing Maceo wanted was to get lost in her beautiful hazel-eyed gaze. He quickly cleared his throat. "So...um...you gon' tell me what the fuck all went down since the last time I saw ya'll?" he asked.

Nikki flinched after Rafael brought the needle through her skin. She drew in a deep breath before releasing the air. "Everything started off smoothly," she told him. "Everything was going as planned. We got in the house...we got the money...shit didn't start fuckin' up until Timothy ended up getting Dre's gun off of him..."

"So he killed Dre?" Maceo asked.

Nikki's lips thinned. Recollecting the events from earlier was just too painful but she struggled to finish the story. "Before I could do anything," she continued. "Someone stormed into the house. We all didn't know what the fuck was going on," Nikki told him. "I mean what are the odds of a home being broken into twice on the same day at the same damn time?"

Maceo listened intently to her story picturing all of the events in his head.

"Anyway when the guy stormed in and demanded for us to drop our guns, Dre started saying how the dude's voice sounded familiar and shit," Nikki explained. "He just kept saying it 'his voice sounds familiar'." Tears pooled in her eyes. "Before I could even put a name to the voice, Hassan turned around and emptied his clip into Dre..." Nikki's voice cracked as she spoke.

"What?" Maceo was completely in disbelief. "Hassan?" He had to be sure that he had heard her correctly. "Hassan? *Hassan*? The nigga you grew up with Hassan?"

Nikki nodded her head. "Yeah...that Hassan," she said in disgust. Just saying his name made her blood boil. "And then the motherfucker had the nerve to turn the gun on me..."

Maceo nodded in understanding. "So that's how you got grazed?"

"Yes," Nikki answered. "That's how it happened."

"You were lucky, ma," Maceo said.

Nikki grimaced and rolled her eyes. "Yeah...well...*his* ass ain't gon' be so damn lucky when I find him."

Maceo ran a hand over his full beard and furrowed his brows. "What do you mean?"

"What do you think I mean?" Nikki asked. "Hassan killed Dre...he tried to kill me...and he took off with all the fucking money," she said through gritted teeth.

Maceo sighed and shook his head. "That shit doesn't sound like Hassan at all...I just can't believe that nigga did that scandalous ass shit."

"Hmph! Well believe it," Nikki said. "And this bullet wound should be enough proof—*Aaahh*! *Dammit*!" Nikki shot daggers at Rafael.

Rafael held his hands up defensively and backed off. "You're all done," he said.

"I just don't understand why Hassan would do some shit like that," Maceo continued. "He always seemed like he was one of those 'I'm down for whatever' type of niggas."

Nikki snorted. "Down for himself. Oh yeah, and his brother," she added.

"Whatchu mean and his brother?" Maceo asked.

"Careem was the mothafucka that stormed into the house," she explained. "They were in cahoots with each other all along. Hassan played Dre and I like pawns in his little game and we fell for the shit."

Maceo shook his head. "Damn. I mean, it wasn't like ya'll saw the shit comin'. This here is some crazy shit," he said. "Fuckery at its worse. It just goes to show how you could know somebody damn near ya whole life, but not know the mothafucka at all."

"Tell me about it," Nikki agreed.

Maceo sighed dejectedly."I can't believe this mothafucka bodied my lil' nigga," he said.

"Without a second thought," Nikki added.

"So what are you gonna do now?" Maceo asked.

"You must not have heard anything I just said," Nikki told him. "I'm gonna find Hassan and make his ass pay—"

"Whoa! Whoa! Whoa! Calm down Kill Bill."

Rafael snickered at the comparison. Nikki quickly cut her eyes at him, and he immediately ceased his laughter.

"Look at what you're wearing? A blood stained jumpsuit," Maceo pointed out. "You're a wanted fugitive. You're gonna stick out like a sore thumb, baby girl. Look, I know you wanna go after this mothafucka," he said. "Shit, after everything you told me I wanna find this nigga and put a bullet in him myself. But you gotta think rationally. And trust me, you can't do this shit on ya own."

Nikki rolled her eyes and looked away. She didn't want to hear it, but Maceo was in fact right. She could not do it on her own. She would either end up dead or apprehended by the authorities.

"Look, just lay low for a lil' while," Maceo told her. "Take a second to just chill you know what I mean?"

Nikki sighed in frustration. She didn't want to waste a second not looking for Hassan because that granted him more time to get away.

"I gotcha back on this one," Maceo added.

Nikki looked over at him. It was not like she had any other options. However, she did not like the idea of having to place what little trust she had left into someone's hands. She had known and trusted Hassan damn near half her life, and he had betrayed her without so much as a second thought.

***

Nikki read the sign of the apartment building they were approaching. The sun was just beginning to set and Nikki had to squint a little to make out the words. "Imperial House. Who lives here?" she asked once they pulled into the complex.

"My baby mama," Maceo answered in a nonchalant tone. "You can lay low here for a lil' while."

Nikki made a face. "Your baby mama?" she repeated in skepticism.

"Well, I would take you to my crib...but my ole lady would trip if I brought home a woman she didn't approve of first."

Nikki cut her eyes in Maceo's direction and smirked.

"I'm just fuckin' with you," he chuckled.

Nikki looked back out her window at the towering apartments located on the shore of Lake Erie. It wasn't too far from the Baxter's home and that fact left an unsettling feeling in the pit of her stomach. She had told Maceo that she wanted to get far away, but right about now she simply had to suck it up and take what she could get.

"So um," Nikki began. "Is your baby mama gonna be cool with you bringin' me here," she asked. "You know how women are..."

"Yo' I ain't even gon' cap. She lightweight gotta lil' attitude problem, but she's cool people," Maceo told Nikki. "You can stay here 'til we figure some shit out."

Nikki sighed dejectedly and rolled her eyes. "Great," she said sarcastically.

"Let me just talk to her," he said.

Five minutes later Nikki stood behind Maceo while he pounded on the wooden door of apartment unit #24.

"Damn, I'm comin' I'm comin'. Stop bangin' on my got damn door like you pay the bills here!" A female's voice shouted on the other end of the door.

Maceo turned and looked at Nikki who rolled her eyes in response.

"Quita, come on. Open the damn door," Maceo said growing a little agitated. He used to have the keys to his baby mother's apartment four lock changes ago.

Seconds later, the door swung open. A pretty dark skinned woman stood in the doorway. She instantly reminded Nikki of actress Tika Sumpter. She wore a white spaghetti strap top and a pair of black jogging shorts. On her feet was a pair of Nike Shox.

Nikki's eyes wandered over her shoulder to the treadmill in the farther corner of the living room. Apparently, Maceo and Nikki had just interrupted her workout session.

"What the fuck is this?" Quita asked looking from Maceo to Nikki. Her gaze connected with the dried blood on Nikki's jumpsuit, and she made a face in disgust. Maceo never ceased to amaze her.

Maceo stepped around Quita and invited himself in. "Quita, this is my home girl, Nikki," he said.

Nikki stepped into the apartment behind Maceo. Quita never took her eyes off Nikki. As expected, she wasn't digging her presence there.

"She needs a place to lay low for a lil' while," Maceo continued. "So I told her she could stay here."

Quita finally tore her gaze away from Nikki in order to give Maceo a look of astonishment. "What?!" she asked with much attitude.

"Oh yeah, and I do pay the mothafuckin' bills here," Maceo added in serious tone. "Don't forget that shit. Nikki gon' head and make yourself comfortable," he said.

Nikki could clearly see that a heated argument was brewing so she quickly made her way towards the living room several feet away.

Quita propped her hands on her narrow hips. “Nigga you must’ve bumped ya mothafuckin’ head somewhere. You just can’t roll up in my damn house tellin’ me that I gotta let a stranger live here. That’s what the fuck motels are for. Like you said nigga, you pay the bills here, than buy that bitch a hotel room.”

Nikki looked over her shoulder and narrowed her eyes at Quita. She knew damn well Nikki had heard the comment, but frankly she didn’t care.

Quita turned towards Nikki. “Um…excuse me. Don’t sit ya ass on my furniture please with those dirty ass clothes.”

Nikki was fuming inside. She didn’t appreciate the way Quita was speaking. She was tempted to jump on top of the white contemporary sectional and start mushing the soles of her sneakers into the fabric. Either that or hit Quita in her damn mouth. The latter sounded like a much better option. Instead of doing either, Nikki propped a hand on her hip and stood there. She was upset that Maceo had even brought her there. It was obvious that Quita didn’t want her there and she had no problem voicing her opinion.

“Quita,” Maceo barked in a deep tone. “First of all, I told you about yo’ mothafuckin’ mouth. That shit is gon’ get you in a world of trouble. Second of all, you got more than enough space here to let her stay—”

"And you gotta whole fuckin' house!" Quita argued. "Why the hell can't Vicki stay with you?"

"Nikki," she corrected Quita. "My name is Nikki."

Quita tossed Nikki a nasty look. "I wouldn't give a damn if your name was Oprah." She turned her attention back to Maceo. "She ain't stayin' here. Flat out."

"Maceo, it's obvious that I'm not welcome here," Nikki finally said. "And I'm damn sure not about to beg or kiss anyone's ass," she added. "I'm out of here."

Quita waved her fingers. "Bye bye then," she said in a sarcastic tone.

Nikki sucked her teeth, and shook her head as she made her way towards the door. *It was a big mistake even coming here,* she thought to herself. Quita's attitude was the last thing she needed.

"Nikki, hold on for a second," Maceo spoke up.

Nikki ignored him as she opened the door and stepped into the hallway. Maceo was hot on her heels. He reached for her elbow, and Nikki had no choice but to stop.

Maceo stood at six foot four inches tall and towered over Nikki's petite frame. He was also stocky and chiseled from a daily workout regimen. Nikki looked up at Maceo and stared into his attractive eyes. She had never noticed how handsome he was until now.

Maybe because she had never looked at him any longer than two seconds.

Shaking those thoughts from her head, she said, "Ya baby mama doesn't want me here and I'm not about to stand there and keep letting her insult me. I was nice the first couple of times, but I refuse to take any more without saying some ignorant shit back. You know me," Nikki said. Had Quita not been Maceo's baby mama, she might have slapped her for coming sideways.

"Man, she be trippin' sometimes," Maceo told Nikki. "But trust and believe, she's good people. I wouldn't have brought you here to waste ya time if she wasn't. Just lemme talk to her again. Aight?" he asked.

Nikki folded her arms and pretended to deliberate on the decision. Who was she kidding though? Maceo was the only person trying to help her in her time of need. "Okay," she finally agreed.

Maceo and Nikki then reentered Quita's apartment. She stood in the same spot with her arms folded across her chest and a nasty expression on her face.

"Look, Q," Maceo began in that powerful deep voice of his. "I ain't never asked you for shit and you know that. Anything you and MaKayla need, I make sure ya'll are both taken care of. All I'm asking you to do is let my home girl stay here for a lil' while until I get something else set up for her," he explained.

"Okay, okay, okay. Damn," Quita finally agreed. "She can stay here. Happy?" She looked over at Nikki and rolled her eyes. Although she wasn't crazy about the idea of allowing another woman to temporarily reside in her home, Maceo did support her and his daughter with no problems. It was more than a lot of men did for their baby mothers and children.

"And can you give her something comfortable to change into?" Maceo turned towards Nikki. "I'm gon' run and grab you a couple things, aight?"

"Hold up," Quita cut in. "First you want her to stay here. Then you want me to give her some damn clothes. What's next? You gon' have our daughter callin' her mama?"

Nikki rolled her eyes. *This chick...*

"Quita," Maceo said. "Chill. For real."

Quita folded her arms.

"Show some hospitality and stop standin' there poutin' and shit. I'll be back in a couple hours," he said before leaving.

Nikki and Quita stood several feet from each other. There was an uncomfortable silence between the two.

Nikki decided to speak first. "So...um...where's your daughter?" she asked.

Quita turned on her heel and walked away. "Over her grandma's," she answered dryly.

Here we go, Nikki said to herself.

4

Fiona used the sleeve of her jacket to wipe underneath her nose. She sniffled and continued to stare out the passenger window of her silver 2008 Toyota Camry. Fiona could not stand the sight or presence of Hassan after the shit he had pulled. She still was trying to figure out how in the hell he was still in her presence. Instead of pressing charges on his ass—like she should have—she had agreed to let him drive her car around the neighborhood to see if he could find the guy who had stolen his car.

Hassan's jaw tensed as he navigated the car around the neighborhood. He had circled the block several times with no such luck. The shit was irritating the hell out of him, but he would not stop driving until the gas needle landed on empty.

Fiona shifted in her seat and sighed.

Hassan finally took note of her tense behavior. She wanted an apology and he knew it. Reaching over, he lightly touched Fiona's thigh. She flinched at his touch, and even had a brief flashback of him strangling her.

"Relax," Hassan said in a soft tone. "Look...I'm um...I'm sorry about that shit back there," he told her. "I reacted horribly. It was fucked up of me to put my hands on you. I know. But trust me when I say, my life was in that fuckin' car," he told her. "You know how you feel about your crib?" he asked her. "You worked hard for everything in it, right?"

Fiona didn't respond.

"Right?" Hassan repeated.

"Right," Fiona mumbled.

"You put your blood, sweat, and tears into everything you worked hard to obtain," Hassan said. "Well, that's how I felt about that car. And everything in it." he added. "So with that said, put yourself in my shoes. Imagine how it would feel to be stripped away from something so important to you. Picture—"

"I get it, Hassan," Fiona cut him off. "I get your point," she said. "But no amount of excuses is going to make up for you putting your hands on me. *So with that said*, I accept your dry ass apology. So let's just drop the subject already."

Hassan looked over at Fiona. He couldn't say that he wasn't surprised by her reaction. She had every right to be pissed off.

"I really am sorry," he said.

Fiona rolled her eyes and resumed looking out her window.

***

Nikki stepped into the living room where Quita sat on the sofa with her feet propped atop of an ottoman. She was munching on sunflower seeds and watching *The Real Housewives of Atlanta.*

"Ha ha ha!" Quita burst into loud laughter. "Kandi, you a fool girl! Oh, shit," she laughed. "I love this broad."

Nikki felt a hell of a lot better after taking a shower, and changing into something a little more comfortable. Of course, Quita had given her the least appealing clothes she could find in her wardrobe, but beggars could not be choosers in this case.

Quita peeled her eyes off the sixty inch television screen long enough to glance at Nikki entering the living room. Her gaze wandered over Nikki's frame and suddenly she found herself sizing Nikki up.

Quita cracked open a sunflower seed and placed the shell into the astray beside a tightly rolled blunt. "So um," she started. "How do you know Maceo?" It was only fair for her to ask. After all, he had brought this chick up in her house.

Nikki took a seat in the white leather track arm chair across from Quita. She really did not feel like delving into her and Maceo's business acquaintance. Besides, it really wasn't any of Quita's damn business in her opinion.

"We're just friends," Nikki said.

Quita cracked open another sunflower seed and placed the shell into the ashtray. "Just friends, huh?" she asked. Quita wasn't buying that 'just friends' bullshit. There was no way in hell that Maceo was not hitting that shit. She knew Maceo's track record. After all, she was his baby mama.

Quita had fought off plenty of women during her and Maceo's five year stint together, and none of the women had claimed to be 'just friends' with him. *What type of shit is this bitch on,* she asked herself.

Quita placed the bag of sunflower seeds onto the coffee table, and picked up the blunt. "Maceo doesn't have *just friends,*" she said. "Look, Nikki, you ain't gotta front with me. I'm not Maceo's woman anyway." Quita's thick lips pulled into a slight smile. "I mean, he may slide through for some pussy once in a while, but it ain't like there's any feelings involved." She was trying her best to get under Nikki's skin in hopes to get more out of her about her and Maceo's relationship.

Nikki released a breath, and ran her palms down her thighs to her knees. "That's all fine and dandy and everything, but Maceo and I are just friends. Nothing more, nothing less," she confirmed.

Quita was still not buying it. "Well, he sure is doing an awful lot for someone who he's just friends with...there must be *some* form of benefits involved," she hinted.

Nikki was getting sick of Quita's nosey ass. This bitch had some real insecurity issues and it had nothing to do with Nikki. “Maceo was a good friend of my boyfriend’s, aight?” she said in an agitated tone.

Quita raised an eyebrow. “Was?” she asked.

Nikki looked down at the back of her hands. “My dude…he um…he was killed,” she said.

Quita lit the filter of the blunt and took a long drag. “Damn. That’s fucked up.” She really did not sound like she was interested or sympathetic.

“Yeah…it is,” Nikki said nonchalantly. She didn’t want to talk about it anymore, and she hoped Quita wouldn’t have any more questions.

“So um…what was his name?” Quita asked. “I might have known him.”

Nikki was totally taken back by her question. Damn. *How insensitive can you be,* she asked herself.

“Quita…I…uh…I really don’t wanna talk about it, aight?” Nikki said.

Quita sucked her teeth, and quickly copped an attitude. “Damn, I only asked what his name was. I didn’t ask how he got his ass murked.” She was totally insensitive with her response.

“That’s it!” Nikki yelled before jumping to her feet. “I’m out this bitch. I’ll take my chances on the street.”

Quita watched as Nikki stormed out the door. Instead of going after her and giving Nikki a much deserved apology, she simply took another drag of the blunt and resumed watching her favorite reality show.

***

Maceo stepped inside his three bedrooms two bathrooms home nestled in a cul de sac in South Euclid, and immediately noticed something was definitely out of the ordinary. All of the lights were turned off, but his girlfriend Nadia's 2012 Cadillac CTS was parked in the driveway. It was Friday, and typically she spent her evenings dancing at Secrets Gentlemen's Club on the west side of Cleveland. Maceo did not expect for Nadia to be home.

Locking the door behind him, he glanced around the dark living room. "Nadia?" he called out. "You here bay?"

No response.

Maceo pulled out the single cigarette that he had stashed behind his left ear as well as the lighter from his pocket.

He flicked a light switch on and slowly made his way towards his bedroom. "Aye, Nadia?" he called out again.

No response.

Maceo lit the filter of his cigarette and took a short pull. Nadia absolutely hated when he smoked in the house, and often argued that the scent would get stuck on the furniture.

"She must have rode with a friend," Maceo muttered to himself.

Pulling out his cell phone he looked to see if he had received any missed calls from her. Strangely, there were none. After tucking his cell phone into the back pocket of his True Religion jeans, he pushed open his bedroom door...

Outstretched enticingly across Maceo's California king size bed, Nadia lay in a scatter of rose petals wearing nothing but a black bikini style sling shot and a pair of six inch stripper heels.

On either side of the bed was a single candle lit and placed on both nightstands. It was the only light illuminating the dark bedroom. Maceo's silhouette danced on the wall as he stood inches from the bed. Instinctively, he reached for the light switch to get a better look.

"No," Nadia quickly spoke. "Keep the light off, papi," she purred in her sexy Spanish accent.

Maceo watched as Nadia climbed out of the bed. He took another pull on the cigarette and released a thick cloud of smoke through his nostrils. He was so engrossed in the scene before him that he had completely forgotten about the no smoking policy.

"What you got goin' on in here?" he asked with a slight smirk. Nadia sure knew how to surprise a nigga.

She sashayed over towards the stereo system on the dresser. Her round ass bounced and jiggled with each step she took. Every year Nadia received butt injections, and it was well worth the money. In Maceo's opinion, an ass could never be too big.

Tattooed in bold cursive lettering on her left ass cheek were the words: Property of Maceo. They had been on and off for three years and Maceo had eventually left Quita for Nadia. He and Nadia shared a rocky past, but Maceo was a king in her world.

"I've been waiting for you to come home," she whispered seductively.

Maceo put out the cigarette in the lime green plastic ashtray on the dresser. "Is that right?" he asked. His eyebrow rose upward, and a smile played in the corners of his mouth.

After Nadia powered on the CD player, The Weeknd's soulful voice filled the room. Wiz Khalifa's "*Remember You*" played softly.

She's about to earn some bragging rights...

I'm 'bout to give it up, like I been holdin' back all night...

Girl take pride in what you wanna do...

Even if that means a new man every night inside of you...

Nadia began swaying her curvy hips to the melody of the song. Maceo admired his woman's curvaceous figure. She gave new meaning to the phrase coke bottle shape.

Maceo shook his head and chuckled. "You somethin' else girl," he said. His dick was growing harder by the second from the little strip show Nadia was putting on for him.

Nadia was Mexican but had the body of a Brazilian. Her smooth fair skin was flawless and blemish-free. Her natural brown hair was dyed jet black, and added to her exotic beauty.

Nadia's D cup breasts spilled out of the tiny bikini. A pierced nipple even peaked through.

"I see you're not goin' to work tonight, huh?" Maceo asked her.

Nadia danced over towards her man, turned around, and slowly gyrated her massive ass against his crotch. "I'd rather entertain you," she purred.

Maceo backed up against the wall, and allowed Nadia to do her thing. "Damn," he sighed. "Damn, the timing...don't be mad at ya boy...but I gotta roll out boo."

Nadia turned around and flung her arms around Maceo's neck. She then pouted, sticking out her lips pumped with lip collagen. Initially, he had been against the procedure, but the pricey augmentation had her shit looking like Angelina Jolie's. He really couldn't complain.

"So you're telling me you're about to leave all of *this*?" she purred. "You must be crazy," she giggled.

Nadia was the second woman today that had called him crazy. "Bay, I got some business I gotta take care of," he told her. "I really wish I could stay and tear this shit up…I really do. But I gotta somethin' to handle, and you know I ain't wit' no speedy fuck—"

"No," Nadia cut in. "You *need* to handle this. That's what you need to do," she said. She took Maceo's right hand, and brought it down towards her kitty. Slipping the thin material to the side, Nadia guided Maceo's middle finger inside her wet depths.

Maceo closed his eyes, sighed, and reclined his head, savoring the wetness of her pussy. "Damn," he groaned. "You ain't gon' make this shit any easier for me, are you?" His dick throbbed, pressing against the zipper of his jeans.

Nadia didn't respond. She simply pulled out Maceo's finger and slid it inside her warm mouth, sucking off her own nectar.

"Damn, Nadia," Maceo whispered. "You know I love when you do that nasty shit."

Nadia smiled in satisfaction knowing she was about to get her way. She slowly lowered herself at Maceo's waist, and proceeded to unfasten his jeans.

***

Two hours of driving around unfortunately led to nowhere, and sadly Hassan was right back at square one. Broke as hell.

Hassan lay on his back staring up at the popcorn ceiling in Fiona's dark bedroom. He couldn't sleep. He barely could think straight.

Suddenly, Fiona reached down and placed her hand on Hassan's crotch. Bad timing. His penis was flaccid, and his sexual appetite was nonexistent.

Hassan quickly grabbed Fiona's hand and flung it off him. He didn't want to be touched; he didn't even want to be bothered with her presence, but he needed a place to lay his head, and a car to get from point A to point B.

"I ain't thinkin' 'bout any mothafuckin' pussy right now," he hissed. "Hell, that wishful thinkin' is what got my ass into this mess to begin with."

Fiona lay silent as she absorbed his harsh words. Minutes later, she climbed out of bed and stood to her feet. "You know what, Hassan?" she asked. "You're starting to change...and I noticed it well before all this car shit even happened."

Hassan sighed in irritation and turned onto his side, facing his back towards her.

Fiona took the gesture to mean 'kiss his ass' so she sulked and stormed out the bedroom, slamming the door behind herself.

5

Quita opened her door for Maceo, and stepped to the side allowing him entrance. He glanced around the empty living room after Quita closed the door. She knew what was coming before he even asked it.

"Where's Nikki?"

Quita ran her tongue along her inner cheek and sighed. She looked over her French manicured nails to avoid Maceo's intense gaze. "She...uh...she left," Quita muttered. Unfortunately, she had not thought of any plausible explanations to tell him.

Quita was barely audible with her response. "Come again?" Maceo asked.

"That bitch left," she said in a much louder tone. "She said she ain't wanna be here—"

"Quita, what the fuck did you do?" Maceo asked in a stern tone. His eyes bore into his baby mother like lasers.

Quita tossed her hands up defensively. "What? Why you lookin' at me like that?" she asked. "I ain't do shit. She ain't wanna fuckin' be here. How come you think I did somethin'—?"

"'Cause I know you, and I know ya mothafuckin' mouth," he said. "So what did you say—?"

"I ain't say shit, Maceo. I ain't do nothin' to her ass," Quita said. "She just up and left—"

"Quita, I ain't live this long being no fool."

She pouted and folded her arms.

"I'ma ask you again," Maceo began. "What. Did. You. Do." Maceo paused between each word he said. He was giving her one last opportunity to tell the truth.

Quita twiddled with a few strands of her hair, and tried her best to put on an innocent look. She was all too familiar with Maceo's bad temper, and even had a few old bruises as a painful reminder. Maceo was a pretty laid back guy but he would also strong arm a hoe in a heartbeat.

"All I did was ask her about her dude—"

"Quita, all I asked you to do was let my home girl stay here. I ain't ask for you to get all up in her business and shit. Damn!" Maceo's deep booming voice bounced off the apartment unit's wall.

"She didn't leave that long ago," Quita added in a small voice. "You can probably catch her."

Maceo shook his head and turned to leave. Had it been anyone else he may have not given a fuck, but Dre was his boy, and he would be damned if he left his girl stranded when it was obvious that she needed help.

***

After driving around for thirty-minutes, Maceo finally located Nikki hiking up the street. It was nearing ten o'clock, and he knew Nikki had no real destination in mind. Cleveland may have been a small city but the odds of her finding Hassan overnight were slim next to none. There was also the possibility that he was not even in Cleveland. And to make matters worse, she was still a wanted fugitive.

Maceo slowly eased alongside the curb beside Nikki much like he had done earlier. She glanced at the tinted windows of the Chrysler 300 but didn't break her stride.

Maceo rolled the driver window down. "Nikki, come on. Get in the car."

Nikki ignored him as she continued to walk up the street. She was freezing her ass off, but her stubbornness would not permit her to accept his help. Besides, there was no way in hell she was going back to Quita's apartment.

"Nikki—"

"Look, Maceo," she stopped in her tracks and turned towards his car. "I appreciate everything you've done for me so far today. I really do," she told him. "But you don't owe me anything. You don't have to look out for me, okay? I mean, I know Dre was your boy, and you may feel like you're obligated to help me, but you're not."

Maceo shifted his gears into Park. "Nikki, I know you think you got it all figured it out. You think you can handle everything on ya own, but I hate to tell you, you can't, baby girl. Look at you. You ain't gotta coat on yo' back or a destination in mind. Nikki you can't do this shit on yo' own," Maceo said. "Please...come out of the cold and get in the car."

Nikki sighed dejectedly. Tears formed in her eyes, but she quickly blinked them away. Slowly she made her way towards the car and climbed into the passenger seat.

Instead of pulling off right away, Maceo sat there for a second. "I wish you would've called me before you up and left."

Nikki folded her arms and allowed the heat from the car to warm her. "I'm sorry, but I couldn't stand being there another second with that bitch." She immediately looked down, regretting her word of choice. "Sorry," she mumbled under her breath.

"You good," Maceo chuckled. "I been knowin' my baby moms was a bitch for a *long* time. You sayin' it ain't news to me," he said. "So you cool?" he asked in a concerned tone.

More tears pooled in Nikki's eyes but she quickly wiped them away before they spilled over. She cleared her throat and looked down at her hands. "Dre and Hassan," she began. "They were the closest thing I had to family...especially after I lost my mother." Her voice cracked as she spoke. "It's just fucked up that things will never go back to the way they used to be...," she paused. "Dre's gone—and I'm telling you Maceo, you should have seen the look in Hassan's eyes. There was so much hate in his eyes. He had no fuckin' remorse, man. I swear. The shit just threw me for a loop. And then for him to turn the gun on me...," Nikki shook her head. "It was like our friendship didn't even exist—"

"Money changes people, Nikki," Maceo said. "Greed is a powerful thing. But don't worry, karma is a bitch. That nigga will get what's coming to him, straight up."

Nikki turned to face Maceo. "Is he?" she asked. "Is he really? Because the more I think about it, I don't even think I have it in me to kill him...I just...I can't even see me pulling the trigger on him," she confessed. "Even knowing everything that happened...I don't have it in me..."

Maceo looked earnestly at Nikki.

"Is that crazy?" she asked in a low tone.

Maceo shook his head. "Nah, ma," he answered. "That ain't crazy at all. That just means you ain't like him..."

***

Nikki looked around the motel room after stepping in behind Maceo. There were two twin mattresses that sat adjacent to one another. *Right back at the same place I started at,* she said to herself.

"My bad, but this is all they had available right now," Maceo spoke up.

Nikki shrugged and stuffed her hands into the back pockets of her jeans. "It's fine. It's no problem. Really." She was simply grateful to have a place to lay her head.

"Oh wait, I also got somethin' for you," he said. "I'll be right back."

Nikki plopped down onto one of the mattresses and waited for Maceo to return. He did a few minutes later brandishing a couple of shopping bags.

"I didn't know what sizes you wore," Maceo said. "But I tried," he chuckled before placing the bag down on the bed that wasn't preoccupied. "Got you a few things I know you needed."

Nikki stood to her feet and walked over to peer inside the bag. There was a couple pair of jeans, shirts, and a gray Aeropostale hoodie. In the other bag was a variety of hygiene products.

"I'm gon' work on gettin' you that birth certificate and social security card," Maceo told her. "But in the meantime," he dug into the pocket of his jeans and extracted his wallet.

"No," Nikki quickly spoke up.

"Think of it as rainy day money," Maceo said pulling out a small wad of cash. "Shit, you never know what'll happen. This money might come in handy—"

"You've already done enough for me," Nikki said. "I can't take any money from you—"

Maceo slowly grabbed Nikki's hand, placed the money inside her palm, and then gradually closed her hand over it.

"Maceo—"

"Just take it...please," Maceo added.

Nikki sighed. Her lips thinned. Hesitantly, she stuffed the money into the back pocket of her jeans.

"I'm real sorry about the shit my baby mama said too—"

"You don't have to apologize for her," Nikki cut him off. "I'm not even on it anymore. Being pissed off about the shit ain't gon' bring Dre back, you know?"

There was an uncomfortable silence that hung between the two.

Nikki spoke up. "Thanks a lot, Maceo," she said. "For everything."

"You got that," he told her. "Besides if the roles were reversed, Dre would do the same for my ole lady."

***

Nikki turned on her side and struggled to get some much needed sleep that night, but the task was damn near impossible. It wasn't that the mattress wasn't comfy enough to get a good night's sleep, Nikki, however could not get Dre's murder out of her mind.

Suddenly, she heard a suspicious sound coming from right outside her motel door. It actually sounded like someone was trying to get inside.

Nikki quickly sat up in her bed and stared at the door. Anxiety coursed through her veins. As expected, her nerves were on edge.

"Maceo?" she croaked out.

There was no response. However the noises on the opposite side of the door grew louder. Nikki quickly reached towards the nightstand for her pistol, but before she was able to retrieve the weapon, the motel door swung open!

Hassan appeared in the doorway wearing a malicious smile on his face. Without uttering a single word, he raised a semi-automatic pistol and took aim.

"No!" Nikki cried holding her arms up to shield her face.

Tat! *Tat*! *Tat*! *Tat*! *Tat*! *Tat*! *Tat*! *Tat*!

A bullet tore through Nikki's right hand, while several bullets impaled her torso. It felt like the wind had been knocked out of her as she dropped backwards into bed.

Hassan slowly made his way closer to Nikki's bed. His weapon hung loosely at his side.

Nikki lay in bed in a pool of her own dark red blood. Thick blood seeped out of her mouth and ran down her cheek. Tears spilled from her eyes as she slowly accepted her fate.

Hassan stepped beside the bed and stared down at Nikki's motionless body in disgust. Her tear-filled eyes looked up at him.

"How could you do this to me?" she cried.

Hassan smiled devilishly. "Easy." He raised the gun towards her head. "I just pulled the trigger."

POP!

6

Nikki suddenly woke up in a panic-stricken state and sat up in bed. Sweat poured profusely down her face and neck. Never had a nightmare seemed so real, so vivid.

Instinctively, she looked down at her torso. Expectedly, there were no bullet holes lodged in her chest and abdomen.

Nikki's breathing was aggressive and ragged as she slowly came back to reality. Her gaze then wandered over towards the door. Of course there were no mysterious noises coming from the opposite side.

Nikki felt foolish. She felt like a child staring into an open closet door waiting for a monster to manifest from the darkness.

Nikki shook her head and lay back down in bed. After pulling the covers over her body, she reached down and lightly touched her tummy. She was only a month pregnant, and did not know what she would do about the 'situation.' The baby could very well belong to Hassan...but there was also a chance that it could be Dre's...

***

Boop.

Boop.

Boop.

The steady beeps from the heart monitor were the only sounds perceivable in Dre's hospital room. Several hours earlier, he had undergone surgery for the bullets and fragments to be removed.

Outside of Dre's door were two police officers. Their presence was mandatory considering the circumstances. The moment Dre recovered they would haul his ass away to jail. However until then, they would simply have to play the waiting game.

Back in the hospital room, Dre's fingers twitched and his eyelids moved about rapidly as he envisioned Hassan pulling the trigger on him over and over again.

***

Hassan had not gotten an ounce of sleep that night. While his own image haunted the dreams of his two friends, he was laying wide awake in bed. Around five in the morning, he actually got tired of lying in the bed and staring at the ceiling. After grabbing the Mild off the nightstand, he climbed out of bed.

Seconds later, Hassan stepped out onto the front porch of Fiona's house. Cupping his hand over the filter of the Mild, he lit it and took a long drag. He blew the smoke through slightly parted lips and then took a seat on the first step.

Nervously bouncing his right foot up and down, he shook his head in frustration. "Fuck, fuck, fuck," Hassan cursed in a low tone while lightly tapping his hand against his head. "What the hell am I gonna do now?" he asked himself.

***

Nikki cocked the hammer to her pistol and slowly raised it. A steady index finger squeezed lightly on the trigger. With unblinking eyes, she stared straight ahead. Her jaw tensed and her nostrils flared wildly.

The pistol began to tremble in her grasp. "Shit!" she groaned in frustration before lowering her weapon.

Nikki drew in a deep breath and released it. She then raised her pistol again and aimed it at her reflection in the bathroom mirror. She was readying herself for a much anticipated encounter with Hassan.

Suddenly, the sound of the motel door closing grabbed her attention.

"Aye, Nikki? It's me." Maceo called out.

Nikki pulled a t shirt over her head and stepped into the room. Maceo stood several feet away carrying a McDonald's bag.

"I got you some breakfast," he said. His gaze slowly wandered down to the pistol clutched tightly in Nikki's hand.

She looked down at the gun as well, walked over to the nightstand, and placed the gun down. "Thank you," she muttered.

Maceo took a seat on the unused mattress and fished inside of the bag. "I talked to my nigga who be makin' the fake documents and shit."

"Is it going to be a long process?" Nikki asked.

Maceo handed her an Egg and Sausage McMuffin. "It's not gon' happen overnight, baby girl," he told her. "A skilled forger could prolly do it in less than a week and it probably wouldn't be detectable on its face. *But*," he added. "That won't help because the moment someone goes to verify the information, it'll obviously be false and ya ass'll be caught. Creating a false identity that passes the usual tests is much trickier than you think," he explained. "It could take weeks or months of *careful* work by someone who knows exactly what they're doing and how to go about the shit. That's where my homie comes into play. He's gon' get you together," he promised. "But in the meantime you just gotta lay low and have a lil' patience."

Nikki unwrapped the breakfast sandwich. "Do I have any other options?" she asked.

***

Hassan slowly navigated his car through the neighborhood for the seventh time that afternoon. He was determined as ever to locate the son of a bitch who had taken off with his car and over two million dollars in cash and jewelry. Unfortunately, Hassan had yet to come across a red Ferrari drop top. There was no telling where that motherfucker could be by now.

Karma could be such a bitch, Hassan thought to himself.

Bumping Chief Keef's "*Love Sosa*" Hassan took in all of his surroundings, keeping his eyes peeled for the vehicle. He promised himself that when he found the mothafucka who took off in his shit he'd pump his body full of lead. There was no way in hell he was going to let him get away with what he had done.

After getting a taste of what it felt like to take a life, Hassan would damn sure do it again in a heartbeat with little to no remorse.

These bitches love Sosa.

O end or no end.

Fucking with them O boys, you gon' get fucked over.

Rari's and Rovers.

These hoes love Chief Sosa.

Hit him with that cobra, now that boy slumped over.

They do it all for Sosa.

Suddenly, something caught Hassan's eye, briefly taking his attention off the road...

Nikki tightened the hood around her head as she walked up the street. Maceo wanted her to stay in the motel room for her own safety, but she just couldn't do that. Right now she was playing a game of cat and mouse. Nikki was the predator and Hassan was the prey…

Hassan craned his neck as he struggled to identify the woman he had just driven past. Even with a hood pulled low over her head, she still looked incredibly familiar. As a matter of fact, she looked a hell of a lot like Nikki—

BOOM!

Hassan's car smashed into the bumper of a car positioned several feet behind the red traffic light. His upper body instantly jerked forward after the impact, and had it not been for the seatbelt fastened across his chest he may have caused bodily damage to himself.

Nikki quickly turned around after the sound of the loud crash behind her. A gust of wind suddenly blew the hood off her head revealing her identity to the world. Luckily the car accident that had just occurred had everyone's attention. She was totally unaware that the driver in the Toyota Camry was in fact the man she was looking for.

"Shit! Shit! Shit!" Hassan cursed punching the center of the steering wheel. Fiona was going to have a damn fit. How was he going to explain this shit to her?

The driver of the car Hassan had just totaled stepped out. He looked pissed off and ready to dial the police at any given moment. "What the hell is your problem?!" he barked. "Didn't you see the damn red light?!"

Hassan ignored the upset man as he looked out the window at the woman walking up the street. She had just pulled her hoodie on and hopped onto an RTA bus.

"Damn," Hassan mumbled under his breath. "Ain't this some shit..." He may have very well been mistaken, but he could've sworn he had just saw Nikki...

***

Nikki walked into The Spot II bar located on Kinsman Avenue. It was a place that Hassan and Careem frequented regularly. It was still broad daylight, but there were quite a few people inside drowning their sorrows during happy hour.

Nikki pulled the hood low over her head and scanned the crowd. World Class Wreckin' Cru's "*Turn Off the Lights*" was playing to give the small bar an old school vibe.

Not wanting to appear too suspicious, Nikki walked over to the bar and ordered a Corona. She made sure to keep her head low so people wouldn't recognize her.

Posted against the wall towards the back of the bar was a dark skinned man with short dreadlocks standing beside a light skinned stud with a fade. Her left brow was pierced as well as her labret. Both appeared to be in their mid to late twenties. They looked like the type of people who kept their ears to the streets.

Nikki took a sip from her beer and slowly made her way over towards the two. The stud cut her eyes at Nikki as she approached them.

"I'm looking for someone," Nikki said once she reached them.

Dreadlocks looked at Nikki, but didn't respond.

"What?" the stud shouted over the loud music.

"I said I'm looking for someone!" Nikki said in a much louder tone.

The stud shrugged and gave Nikki a nasty expression. "So. The fuck that got to do with us?"

Nikki was slightly taken back by her displeasing tone. She sized the woman up. The stud towered over Nikki's petite frame by an entire foot, but size definitely didn't matter in her eyes. She had dropped plenty of bitches twice her size.

"It doesn't have anything to do with you," Nikki said. "But I was wondering if you might have seen or heard anything about these two people I'm looking for. I can pay you for your time," she added.

The stud's lip thinned as she looked over at her homie.

"Let's go outside and talk so we don't have to be hollerin' over the music and shit," the stud explained.

Nikki agreed and following them both towards the back door. Dreads opened the large, blue metal door and motioned for Nikki to go out first. Fortunately, she was strapped just in case they tried some funny shit.

The stud followed behind Nikki into the narrow alley behind the small bar.

Nikki turned around to face them. "I'm looking—"

WHAP!

Before Nikki could even finish her statement, she was sucker punched by the stud! Uncontrollably, she stumbled backwards after the impact, and dropped the Corona she was holding. The glass shattered upon impact. Dreads suddenly ran up and grabbed Nikki from behind before she was able to retaliate. Her hood quickly fell off her head revealing her face.

7

"Get off me!" Nikki yelled. Blood was smeared all over her pearly white teeth from when she had accidentally bitten down on her tongue. There was also a small cut that had opened on her lower lip. "Get the fuck off me!" Nikki screamed as she thrashed about in Dread's embrace. He was far too strong to fight off.

The stud slowly approached Nikki with a menacing look in her eyes.

"Look, I didn't come to you looking for trouble!" Nikki yelled. Her heart hammered in her chest. As much as she hated to admit it, she was terrified. With the guy's tight grip on both her arms she was unable to reach for her gun.

"Well, bitch you found it," the stud said.

Nikki spit out a mouthful of blood onto the concrete. "Dammit, I'm pregnant!" she yelled hoping they would at least have a little sympathy for her.

The stud snorted. "Bitch, that ain't got shit to do with us," she spat.

"This hoe is cappin' anyway," Dreads spoke up. "Fuck you in here drinkin' for if you pregnant?" he asked.

Nikki tried her hardest to keep from crying, but the tears eventually began to spill over her lids. "Get the fuck off me!" she yelled through gritted teeth.

"You know what?" the stud said smiling mischievously. "You're kinda cute." Without warning, she walked up and pinched the hell out of Nikki's right breast through the thick cotton fabric of her sweatshirt.

"Don't you fuckin' touch me, bitch!" Nikki spat. Her breast throbbed in pain.

"What?! Hoe, you must not know who I am!" She approached Nikki as if she were preparing to strike her.

Nikki tried to kick the woman, but missed. Dreads tightened his grip on her arms, roughly bending them in the process. Nikki yelped in pain.

The stud walked up to Nikki, and Nikki thought she might hit her, but instead she reached into Nikki's front pocket and pulled out the wad of money Maceo had given her last night. She was totally oblivious to the piece Nikki had on her.

"Well, I'll be damned," the stud smiled. "This hoe got a knot on her."

Suddenly, and without warning, Nikki bashed the back of her skull into Dread's nose smashing the bone instantly.

"*Aaahh*! Shit!" he screamed in pain. He immediately released Nikki and went to cradle his bloody and broken nose.

Before either of them was able to attack Nikki, she quickly reached for her waist and pulled out the shiny pistol.

"Fuck! She's strapped!" The stud yelled in surprise before turning on her heel to run. Dreads quickly followed suite.

Nikki cocked the Glock and fired several shots.

POP!

POP!

POP!

POP!

Bullets whizzed past them both and one actually struck the woman in the back of her calf muscle as she fled. She instantly dropped onto the ground several feet from where Nikki stood. Dreads didn't bother going back to help his friend as he continued to run off.

"Aaahh!" she cried out. "She shot me! Somebody help me! This bitch shot me!"

Nikki lowered her weapon and quickly made her way over towards the injured woman on the ground.

With each step Nikki took, the stud's heart beat faster and louder. She just knew Nikki was preparing to put a bullet in her head. However, Nikki's intentions were not to kill her. She actually just wanted her money back.

The back door to The Spot II suddenly swung open seconds before Nikki reached her. Nikki didn't bother turning around to see who it was. She simply took off running in the opposite direction.

***

Nikki wiped away the blood trickling from her lip as she sped walked through the back ways and shortcuts of her old hood. The bitter taste of blood rested on her taste buds. She was fuming mad about the altercation that had just occurred, and the fact that she was barely able to defend herself. She was even tempted to go back and put a bullet in the bitch's head who had robbed her. Even after everything was said and done, Nikki did not even get the money back. How would she explain that shit to Maceo?

Tiny raindrops began to fall as a once bright blue sky quickly turned pale gray. Ironically, the weather matched Nikki's mood. Wind blew aggressively blowing the rain in a diagonal direction.

Somewhere in between walking and silently cursing to herself about the ordeal, Nikki wandered inside a nearby convenience store. Her mind was in complete disarray. Instead of focusing and thinking rationally, she suddenly decided to act on impulse.

Walking up to the counter of the store, Nikki snatched her pistol out and aimed the weapon directly at the Indian cashier. "*Give me all the fuckin' money in the register*!" she screamed.

There was only one customer in the convenience store. The young, black woman shrieked in fear and ducked behind the nearby chips stand. Never in her wildest dreams would she have thought that she may possibly lose her life over a 20 oz. Pepsi.

The cashier tossed his hands up defensively. Regardless of Nikki asking for the money that was always the first thing cashiers did whenever a gun was pointed in their faces.

"*The money*!" Nikki barked.

Ding!

The bell above the store's door chimed signaling that someone had just entered the store. Nikki turned to her left and watched as a white subcontractor worker stepped inside. He froze in place at the sight of the weapon in Nikki's hand.

Suddenly, she noticed the cashier move from the corner of her. Everything seemingly occurred in slow motion. The Indian cashier retrieved the twelve gauge shotgun underneath the counter, quickly pumped the forend of the gun, and took aim.

Instinctively, Nikki ducked down a second before the cashier pulled the trigger.

BOOM!

The loud sound of the gun blast rang throughout the small convenience store. Pellets tore through the beverage cooler's glass in the back of the store.

"*Aaaaahhhh*!" the female customer screamed before lying flatly on the grimy floor. She shielded her head with her hands and said a silent prayer that she would make it out of this alive.

The cashier started to pump the shotgun a second time before he realized his shells were in the back office buried inside the bottom drawer of his desk. Tossing the useless gun, he ran around the counter and prepared to deal with Nikki using his fists.

Nikki's heart pounded ferociously in her chest.

What the fuck did I get myself into, she asked herself.

Nikki could barely think straight, but luckily she knew enough to get the hell out of the store. Either that or deal with the repercussions. Darting towards the exit, she was unexpectedly tackled by the worker who had entered the store seconds ago.

She fell backwards, smacking the back of her head against the hard floor. Her pistol landed several feet from her body.

Fucking captain save a hoe, Nikki thought.

Before she was able to catch her breath, the cashier snatched the hoodie of her sweatshirt, viciously choking her in the process.

"Call the police now!" he ordered in his thick accent. "I got her! She isn't going anywhere!"

Nikki reached for her throat. Her air supply was completely shut off as her own hood choked her to death. Tears welled in her eyes. Her feet kicked and scraped against the floor as she fought to draw in air.

The subcontractor stood to his feet and pulled out his cell phone as the Indian cashier continued to purposely choke Nikki.

8

“Aye! What the fuck you doin,’ man?!” Two young black guys suddenly entered the store.

They didn’t see a robber being apprehended or justice being served. Instead they saw an Indian man harming an innocent black woman while a white man stood nearby doing nothing to help.

“Get the fuck away from her!”

Before the cashier was able to explain what was happening, the two guys charged full speed and attacked him. He had no choice but to relinquish his hold on Nikki as he proceeded to defend himself against the vicious blows being inflicted. In the midst of the fight that had just broken out, Nikki hurriedly darted out of the convenience store.

It wasn’t until she made it around the corner that she realized she had left her gun behind. Her finger prints were all over the weapon, but there was no way in hell she was going back to retrieve it.

***

“I only had liability,” Fiona stated in an agitated tone. Her arms were folded tightly across her chest and all her weight was shifted to one leg. Pissed off would have been an understatement. She was fuming mad over the car accident.

"Look man, it was an accident," Hassan said nonchalantly. "When I find the nigga that took my whip and get it back, I'll pay to get ya car fixed ASAP. You got that," he told her.

Fiona dropped her arms at her side and shook her head in frustration. Her sleek, tight long ponytail shook in the process. "Hassan, why do you keep trying to look for the mothafucka yourself?" she finally asked. "Why not just report the shit and let the police handle it—"

"I don't want to get the police involved, aight?" he cut her off.

"Scared they might find something they shouldn't?" Fiona challenged.

Hassan cut his eyes at her. Fiona was as sexy as she wanted to be, but she could definitely get her cute ass slapped up if she continued talking reckless. Besides, Hassan wasn't in the mood. "Mind ya business," he stated in a flat tone.

The corners of Fiona's mouth pulled back as her eyes narrowed. "You're right," she said. "I should have minded my own business. I should never have gotten involved in yours, maybe my mothafuckin' car wouldn't be totaled right now."

Hassan decided to let Fiona vent about the shit instead of going tit for tat with her. Plopping down on her living room sofa, he pulled out a Black N Mild and proceeded to freak it. Fiona's car was the last thing on his mind...and Nikki just so happened to be the first.

What the hell is she still doing in Cleveland, he thought to himself.

Fiona continued to rant and rave until her cell phone began ringing.

"Saved by the mothafuckin' bell," Hassan muttered under his breath before firing up the Mild.

"Yeah, girl I can still do your hair. Come on over," Fiona said exasperatedly. "And don't forget the hair glue, I don't have anymore."

Hassan took a long drag before releasing the smoke through his nostrils. *Cleveland is such a small ass city,* he thought to himself.

***

Nikki stood directly in front of the flat screen television engrossed in the news story broadcast. She pressed a warm washcloth against her swollen lip. Her face throbbed in pain, but the aching was the last thing on her mind as she stared at her own mug shot plastered on the flat screen TV.

After the news reporter gave a brief description of what had happened during the robbery, they revealed the mug shots of both men who had come to her rescue. Had it not been for them, Nikki would've probably ended up on some mortician's metal slab.

Suddenly, the sound of the motel door closing grabbed her attention. She turned and watched as Maceo entered the small room. He wore a look of irritation and disappointment. He had just heard the news story being broadcasted on 107.9 during his ride to the motel.

Maceo wanted to go ham on her about the shit she had pulled, but he softened a little at the sight of her bruises.

Instead of Nikki taking Maceo's advice about lying low, she had chosen to do the exact opposite. She was drawing attention to herself in the worst possible way.

Maceo folded his buff arms across his massive chest. "You just couldn't listen to me and fall back, huh?" he asked.

"Maceo—"

"Look, I can't help you if you can't help ya damn self," he said clearly agitated.

Nikki sighed and walked over towards the bed before plopping down on the mattress. She could not even think of a legitimate reason for why she had done the shit she did. "I'm sorry," she said looking down at her hands.

Maceo snorted. "Sorry?" he repeated sarcastically. "You doin' dumb shit on impulse gon' get you fucked up Nikki—it's gon' get me fucked up!"

Nikki looked up at Maceo. He was not hiding the fact that he was pissed off. "Maceo, you don't understand—"

"Nikki, you ain't the only one pissed off about the shit Hassan did. Dre was my homie. And I'm tryin' to do right by you," he told her. "But how am I gonna be able to get you out of all this if I'm locked up and you dead somewhere because you doin' shit without thinkin' first?"

Nikki rolled her eyes and sighed in frustration.

Maceo slowly walked over towards Nikki, knelt down before her, and took her hands in his. "Look, I ain't tryin' to blow down on you or no shit like that. But I got ya best interest at heart. Believe that. All I'm askin' you to do is just fall back, chill, and let me handle everything, aight?"

Maceo's large hands were warm and comforting as he held Nikki's small hands in his. His soothing touch let her know that everything was going to be okay despite everything. It also had her cheeks flushing and her face warming up. His Gucci cologne was strong and inviting.

Their eyes met...

"You gotta meet me halfway," Maceo told her. "You got to..."

Nikki nervously cleared her throat and slipped her hands out of Maceo's. "I can do that," she nervously croaked out. Her voice was barely above a whisper. *Get it together girl,* she told herself.

***

Long, slender fingers tapped against a wooden oak desk as a man stared at the mug shot of the young, brown-skinned woman on his fifty-two-inch flat panel TV. The media had labeled her 'dangerous' and 'a threat to society'. News reporters had warned citizens that if they saw Nikita Brown not to try to apprehend her but instead to notify authorities immediately.

Lexer slowly reached for the remote control on his office desk and turned the television off. He had already seen enough.

A body guard was positioned in the farthest corner of his office. A man like Lexer never went unprotected since he had his share of enemies like most 'business men'.

Lexer stood at six feet five inches tall and was very slender in frame. He was ball-head, his skin was the color of coal, and his beady eyes had an unsightly yellow tint to them. There was a small moon shaped scar on his left cheek from when he was stabbed in prison over twenty years ago.

Lexer was a very intimidating man, and it was not just because of his appearance. It was because of the horrific things he could make happen with a mere snap of one of his bony fingers. He was a cold-hearted killer without ever having to shed blood himself.

He was also a loan shark, and his ethics were a lot different than most illegal moneylenders. Instead of using blackmail or repetitive threats to enforce repayments, Lexer used more unorthodox methods.

Lexer picked up his cell phone and dialed the number of a trustworthy informant. “Find out any and everything you can on a Nikita Brown.” His voice was deep, calm, and raspy and sounded eerily similar to actor Tony Todd.

Lexer disconnected the call. Now it was time to play the waiting game.

Unbeknownst to Hassan, Nikki, and Dre, Timothy Baxter was one step away from filing bankruptcy. His home and vehicles were purchased on loan credit, and he even went as far as to stash the last of his money inside a hidden safe to keep the bank from taking it. In a desperate attempt to keep his mansion from being seized, Timothy borrowed a hefty loan from Lexer.

Unfortunately, Timothy was now dead, and Nikki was quickly fingered as the culprit. In other words, Nikki now had something else to worry about other than being apprehended by the police.

9

Hassan had just come from using the bathroom, and was on his way back into the living room when he overheard Fiona's friend, Sasha talking about him. He stopped mid-stride and stood out of view in order to eavesdrop.

"How and why the fuck is you lettin' that nigga stay here after he crashed ya shit up like that? Hell, why is he even here period? What is he homeless or somethin'?" she asked.

Sasha sat on a wooden chair at the dining room table while Fiona stood over her doing an invisible part quick weave.

Hassan folded his arms across his chest and twisted his mouth up. He really wanted to hear everything their asses had to say. Both women were completely oblivious to his presence.

"I don't know," Fiona answered truthfully. "I haven't asked him." She trailed a small portion of hair glue along a single track and pressed it against Sasha's scalp.

"Well, what the fuck is he doing for you?" Fiona's friend asked. "'Cause you told me a while ago all ya'll do is fuck. I mean, shit you can get dick anywhere, Fi. And that's real."

Fiona knew there was truth to what Sasha was saying but it was actually more to it. She did not want Hassan there, but truthfully she was too afraid to tell him to leave. She still had nightmares about him strangling her in the middle of the street in broad day light. That event was something Fiona did not care to share with her friend, Sasha...or anyone else for that matter.

Sasha sucked her teeth. "Look all I'm tryin' to say is you need to kick that lame ass nigga out and take his ass to court," she said with much sass.

This bitch doesn't even know me, Hassan thought to himself. He was two seconds from storming into the dining room and slapping Sasha's big mouth ass.

"I don't wanna do all that," Fiona said. "He's already goin' through enough since his car got stolen and shit."

Sasha sucked her teeth again. That annoying sound was irking Hassan's last nerves.

"Oh, his car this, his car that!" Sasha said sarcastically. "All this bullshit with his car. Any nigga with common sense would have just contacted the police and been done with the shit. It's obvious there's some shit in it that he don't want the cops to find. Or better yet the nigga that stole the car since he got you scourin' the city with his ass. Fi, I'm tellin' you, that nigga is on some real shit. You better get rid of his ass—

That was it! Hassan had heard more than enough. Suddenly, and just as unexpectedly he burst into the dining room in a fit of rage.

"Bitch, you gotta roll out!" Hassan yelled.

Before Sasha was able to respond, he snatched a handful of her partially done hair and yanked her out the wooden chair she sat in. His anger had him behaving impulsively, but he would be damned if he stood around and let this nobody ass bitch continue to talk shit.

"Hassan, what are you doing?!" Fiona screamed.

"*Get the fuck off me*!" Sasha screamed. She struggled to stand to her feet even with Hassan's hand wrapped tightly around her hair. Uncontrollably, she stumbled back onto the floor. Tracks painfully tore from her hair, and glue peeled from her scalp as Hassan proceeded to drag Sasha through Fiona's house and towards the front door.

"Hassan, get the hell off of her! *Are you fuckin' crazy*?!" Fiona screamed.

Sasha kicked her feet wildly and scratched at Hassan's hands as he mercilessly dragged her across the carpeted floor. Her jeggings slid partially down exposing her bare ass. The carpet burned her skin due to the friction.

"*Aaaahhhh*!" Sasha cried out in pain. "*Let go of me*!"

"Nah, bitch you gotta go! You done overstayed yo' mothafuckin' welcome!" Hassan yelled.

"You're acting crazy, Hassan!" Fiona yelled following after them but making sure to keep a safe distance. She really wanted to intervene and help her girl, but she didn't want to risk getting her ass kicked. It was apparent that Hassan had lost his damn mind.

Once Hassan reached the front door, he slung it open and all but tossed Sasha onto the rickety porch.

Sasha was in tears and her hair was in complete disarray. Mascara leaked down her light brown cheeks, and her clothing was halfway on. She had come into Fiona's home looking halfway decent, and now she looked an utter mess.

Sasha struggled to pull her jeggings up as she stood to her feet. "You crazy son of a bitch!" She wiped the mucus from underneath her nose. "*Fuck you*!"

Hassan clenched his fists and advanced on Sasha. "Bitch, you better get the fuck outta here 'fore I really beat ya ass!" he threatened.

Sasha flinched and quickly backed away from Hassan. She had never been so afraid in her entire life. There was something animalistic in Hassan's eyes.

Even in her state of fear, Sasha continued to shout out meaningless threats. "How dare you put your hands on me, motherfucker!" She accidentally stumbled down the porch's steps as she screamed at Hassan. "I'ma be back with my baby daddy!" she threatened. "You just watch nigga! You got the right one!"

Hassan stepped down two steps. "Bitch, I'm givin' ya ass three seconds to roll out."

Sasha backed away but kept her gaze focused on Hassan. Fiona suddenly appeared in the doorway with a helpless expression on her face.

"Ya boy is fuckin' crazy, Fiona! You need to leave his ass alone!" she warned her friend. "He gon' get you fucked up, watch!"

"*Three*!" Hassan counted. "*Two*!"

Sasha hurried towards her Volkswagen, climbed in, and stuck her middle finger up at Hassan from behind the windshield. Satisfied with her gesture, she quickly pulled out of Fiona's driveway and skirted off.

Hassan turned around and noticed Fiona standing in the doorway with tears rolling down her cheeks. Shaking her head, she asked, "What the hell is wrong with you, Hassan? You ain't the same nigga I met in the club," she said in a low tone.

"You're right," he said. "I'm not..."

***

Maceo knocked loudly on his baby mother's door and waited patiently for her to answer. He had just left the motel with Nikki, and thought about dropping by Quita's home to see what she was up to. Hell, who was he kidding? He wanted some pussy. As odd as it seemed, Nikki had left that effect on him, and they had spent no more than five minutes in each other's presence.

Maceo had forced himself into believing that he was simply helping out a friend of a friend. Nothing more, nothing less. He was also forcing himself to not look at Nikki like that. After all, she was his nigga's girl, but he'd be lying to himself if he did not find her remotely attractive. She was cute, petite, and feisty.

However, circumstances would not permit him to push up on Nikki regardless of his manly instincts. *I'm not that type of nigga*, he kept telling himself. Nikki was counting on him to be there for her, and sticking his dick in her was going to help her in the least.

Several seconds later, the door opened and Quita appeared wearing a silk pink robe. There was a light amount of sweat on her neck and chest, but Maceo doubted she had just finished a workout.

"Um...M—Maceo," she stuttered tightening the sash to her robe.

Maceo barged into her home. "Fuck goin' on in here?" he asked with a slight attitude. "You got company or something?"

Quita looked flustered. It was apparent that she had just been caught off guard.

"'Cause you know better than to have some mothafuckin' niggas around my daughter."

"Maceo, MaKayla is at ya mama's, remember?" she asked.

Maceo quickly made his way through Quita's apartment. The living room was the first area he checked.

Quita followed after Maceo like a teenage daughter fearful of her father catching a guy in her bedroom. "Maceo, what are you doing?" she asked breathlessly. "You can't just be—Maceo, no!"

It was far too late. Maceo's hand was already wrapped around the doorknob leading into Quita's bedroom. He pushed the door open, and as expected, found a half-naked guy lying in his baby mama's bed.

"Maceo," Quita began.

"Aye, who the fuck is you?" Quita's boy toy asked.

Maceo turned towards Quita who stood in the doorway with a look of fear in her eyes.

"I know you ain't got no nigga up in this bitch, like he the one who pay bills here," Maceo said. "Like he *deserves* to be here or some shit."

"What?!" Quita's male friend asked with an attitude. "Mothafucka, who are you?!"

Maceo cracked his neck bones without even having to use his hands. "Nigga, I'ma give yo' ass two seconds to bounce," he warned the guy.

Quita's friend jumped out of the bed. "Or what?" he asked. Suddenly, he felt foolish standing up to a man who towered over him by an entire foot and outweighed him by at least a hundred pounds.

"Trust me homie. You don't wanna find out," Maceo warned him with clenched fists.

Quita's friend backed up and shook his head. "I ain't 'bout to fight over no chick," he said. He was simply using that as an excuse to punk out. "I'm gone," he said collecting his clothes.

Less than a minute later, the front door closed.

Quita tossed her hands up. "Damn, Maceo," she whined. "How many damn times you gon' run my men up outta here?" she asked.

"However many times I got to until you learn," he told her.

"I ain't ya girl," Quita said. "You know that."

Maceo' jaw muscle tensed signifying that he was irritated. "You know how I feel about you bringing men up in here where my daughter lays her head."

"She's not even here, Maceo. Damn. Sometimes I need a moment for myself to just do *my* thing," Quita said.

Maceo smirked and snorted. "Do yo' thing, huh?"

Quita used her hands to emphasize her words. "Yes. Do my thing," she said. "And why yo' ass even here? Shouldn't you be at home laid up with Buffie the *fake ass* body?"

Maceo sucked his teeth and took a seat on Quita's mattress. "I don't feel like being bothered with that bitch right now," he said. "I can't even spend an hour with this hoe without her talkin' me to death about some new type of surgery she wanna do to herself," he complained.

Maceo loved Nadia to death, but it was obvious that she had some serious issues with her self-esteem and image. Nadia often blamed it on her Body dysmorphic disorder, but Maceo thought it was deeper than just that.

"Maceo, you knew that bitch was self-conscious when you first met her ass," Quita said matter-of-factly. "Quit frontin'. This new hoe must got ya ass wantin' some new shit," she hinted.

"New hoe?" Maceo asked quizzically.

Quita undid her robe, and let it drop around her bare feet. She wore only a pair of purple lace panties. The color looked great on her chocolate complexion.

"You know who I'm talkin' bout," she said. "Vicki..."

Maceo chuckled. "Nikki."

Quita walked over towards the bed. "Whatever."

"What do you mean she got me wantin' some new shit?" Maceo asked.

Quita sucked her teeth. "I saw the way you were lookin' at her yesterday. All soft and shit. 'Nikki, wait. Hold on. Don't leave'," she mimicked Maceo's voice sarcastically.

"Shut up," Maceo laughed.

Quita slid in between Maceo's legs and proceeded to unfasten his jeans.

"It ain't like that. Real talk," Maceo said.

Quita unzipped Maceo's jeans. "Then what is it like?" she asked. "You come in here today talkin' shit about ya girl, but just yesterday you was cool with her fake ass booty and double D breasts," she said. "I think ole girl Nikki got you lustin' over those A cups," Quita teased.

"Nah, they C cups at the most," Maceo corrected her.

Quita slapped the hell out of Maceo's bicep. "See!" she laughed. "I knew ya'll wasn't just friends!"

"Swear on everything we are, Q. It ain't like that. She was my nigga's girl," he explained. "I'm helping her out on the strength that if I got killed, my nigga Dre would've been there for you and Kay."

Quita stared into Maceo's eyes and listened.

"My dude Dre kept a nigga eatin'. He was cool peoples," Maceo explained. "So I'm just lookin' out. That's all."

Quita's full lips pulled into a smile. "Well that is so sweet of you, bay," she said. "But are we gon' fuck or what?"

***

BOOM!

BOOM!

BOOM!

Hassan already knew who the person on the opposite end of the door was, and he had actually expected him to show up sooner or later.

An hour had elapsed since Hassan had tossed Sasha out on her ass, and she damn sure kept her promise about returning with her baby daddy.

Terrance pounded ferociously on Fiona's front door while Sasha sat safe and sound in the passenger seat of her '08 Volkswagen Jetta.

Terrance stood at six feet two inches tall and was fairly slender in frame. He was brown skinned and had no visible hair on his face, and was often mistaken to be younger than his thirty years of age.

Sasha watched from inside the vehicle, hoping and waiting for Hassan to cut up on her baby daddy so she could witness him get his ass whupped. She was seething inside about the way he had manhandled and dogged her earlier, and she was even more pissed that her girl, Fiona had stood by and did nothing.

"Come on bitch, open the door," Sasha mumbled underneath her breath.

BOOM!

BOOM!

BOOM!

Terrance continued to pound on the front door. "Nigga, I know ya ass in here! Open the mothafuckin' door!" he yelled.

Hassan took his time as he slowly made his way towards the door. "When are these mothafuckas gon' learn I'm not the one?" he asked himself.

Doe Boy's "Boyz N Da Hood 2" blared from the speakers in Fiona's living room. Thick clouds of smoke hung in the air. Hassan had smoked the last of Careem's kush, and was high out of his mind and ready for whatever.

I ain't no killer, but don't push me.

You can call me anything you want just make sure it ain't pussy.

Won't let 'em catch me lackin', I ain't tryin' to catch a bullet.

I put that on my fuckin' grave, you run up, I'ma pull it.

"Hassan, please don't open the door," Fiona pleaded. "They'll go away. You ain't got shit to prove—"

"You done?" Hassan asked irritated. His eyes were glazed over and red-rimmed, and his lids were low. "I suggest you back up."

Fiona rolled her eyes and stormed off, sulking to herself.

"Open the mothafuckin' door!" Terrence hollered from outside. "You wanna put ya hands on my chick, then fight me nigga! Open the door!"

Hassan unlocked the bolt, twisted the doorknob, and reached behind his back for his piece...

10

Obviously Terrance was only 'cutthroat' when he talked shit, because as soon as Hassan shoved the gun in his face, he instantly shut up.

Instinctively, Terrance raised his hands up defensively as he backed up. He kept his gaze locked on the barrel of the gun.

He swallowed the large lump that formed in his throat. "Come on nigga, you ain't gotta do this shit," he pleaded.

Hassan took slow steps towards Terrance. It was pitch black outside, and there were only a few street lights lit on Fiona's street. *I wonder how many witnesses there would be if I popped this fool right here right now,* he thought to himself.

"You were talkin' that big shit, nigga," Hassan said keeping his gun aimed at Terrance's head. "Talk that shit now."

"Um…I…uh…" Terrance swallowed again, never taking his eyes off the gun. He didn't expect for Hassan to be strapped. "Look, I don't want no trouble, man," he said.

"Nigga, you brought the trouble here," Hassan said. "So you must want somethin'!"

Terrance accidentally tripped and stumbled down the stairs as he backed away from Hassan.

Hassan cocked the hammer, and Terrance nearly pissed himself!

Sasha watched the entire scenario unfold. Her heart hammered rapidly in her chest. With each second that passed, she feared Hassan would actually pull the trigger on her man.

"I don't want no trouble," Terrance repeated. He was totally shaken up.

"Then I suggest you get ya ass back in ya car and roll out. And don't let that bitch talk you into comin' back 'cause next time..." Hassan waved the gun. "I'm bustin. Straight up."

Terrance quickly took off towards his car, stumbling as he ran. After regaining his footing he jumped into the driver's side. Apparently, his nerves were so bad that he barely could drive since he pulled out of the driveway crookedly, slightly running over the lawn in process.

Hassan shook his head as he watched Terrance disappear out of sight. "It's crazy how a quick nigga crumbles when he got a gun in his face," he said to himself.

***

"*Oooohh*! Fuck! I missed this dick!" Quita moaned.

Maceo had one leg hoisted up on the bed while he stood upright, gripping Quita's small waist. His pelvis slammed against her round ass with each powerful stroke he inflicted.

"I can't tell," Maceo said breathlessly. "That nigga be diggin' in this shit like me?" he asked. Maceo absolutely loved to talk shit during sex.

Quita's cheeks flushed as she felt a powerful climax approaching. "Don't nobody beat it like you daddy," she whimpered.

Bands a make her dance.

Bands a make her dance.

All these chicks poppin' pussy, I'm just poppin' bands.

Maceo's iPhone suddenly rang on the nightstand.

"Please don't stop," Quita pleaded. "I'm almost there."

"Damn, Q. This might be some money though," he said pulling away.

Quita sucked her teeth and dramatically flopped onto the bed as Maceo went to answer his phone. The number displayed on his screen did not look familiar. He would have ignored the call had he not assumed the caller might have been Nikki.

"Yo?" he answered.

Quita watched Maceo's brows furrow as he carefully listened. She then reached down and proceeded to play with her clit. "Come on, baby," she purred.

Maceo held up his index finger signaling silence. "Aight. Gimme a half an hour, and I'ma hit you back," he said before disconnecting the call.

"Don't tell me you're about to leave," Quita said with a look of disappointment in her eyes.

"I got moves to make," Maceo said as he began to dress.

Quita sucked her teeth. "I guess," she said reaching towards her nightstand. "I could've kept ole dude here for all this," she mumbled under her breath.

Maceo buttoned his True Religion jeans. "Don't get fucked up," he warned Quita.

"You're such a fuckin' control freak, Maceo," Quita told him. "It's cool for you to have a bitch, but I can't have any niggas up in my own house?"

"Not unless those mothafuckas are payin' the bills in this bitch," he told her. "And last I checked I did that shit. So I'm the only nigga that should be swimmin' in that," he pointed to Quita's shaved kitty.

Quita produced a pink vibrating dildo from the nightstand drawer. "Last *I* checked, I had a second option," she teased.

***

Maceo made his way down a dark and damp alley. Dressed in all black, he wore a black leather baseball jacket, a pair of black Levis, and keeping his bald head warm was a black skully. He looked both intimidating and sexy at the same time.

He had two of his homies with him for protection just in case any funny shit popped off. He did not have time to fuck around with any stick up kids, undercover cops, and all the other bullshit that came with hustling.

"This that shit right here, Maceo said pointing to a gun. His pride and joy. "Saiga-12. Automatic shot gun. Twenty rounds in 3.3 seconds." Maceo lifted the gun up. "And you ain't gettin' this shit nowhere else. I guarantee you that." He aimed the gun at his potential buyer. "You see the infrared beam?"

Terrance tensed up a little. This was the second time tonight a gun had been aimed at him.

His cousin had put him onto Maceo, saying that he was the only cat in Cleveland who could get him fire at a reasonable price. Terrance had Maceo's number stored in his cell phone for quite some time, but never thought to use it until now.

Terrance felt like his entire manhood had been insulted. Not only had he been punked by some young thug in the streets, but his baby mother had witnessed it. Terrance had fled like a dog with its tail tucked between his legs, but now he was ready to come back bustin'.

Terrance swallowed the lump that had formed in his throat. “Yeah, that infrared shit slick,” he said. “But do you got anything...I don’t know...a lil’ less creative...?”

Maceo turned towards one of his homies. “Hand me that PS90, my nigga.”

Terrance’s eyes widened at the sight of the impressive firearm.

“The PS90 got extremely low recoil. It never misses its target,” Maceo promised.

Maceo absolutely loved guns. It was the only thing he could honestly say he loved more than women. He had inherited the love of guns from his father who was once an avid hunter. Oddly enough, Maceo’s father was murdered during a carjacking when Maceo was only twelve. He had died at the hands of the object he loved the most.

“This that shit right here,” Maceo said. He aimed the gun into the dark shadows of the alley several feet away and began firing.

BOOM!

BOOM!

BOOM!

BOOM!

Maceo chuckled as he fired off the shots. "You see that shit?" he asked Terrance before handing the gun back to his homie.

"Yeah, that was straight," Terrance answered. "But what else you got?"

Maceo's expression became serious. "Assault rifles, revolvers, shot guns, semi-automatics, handguns. I got whatever you need, my nigga," Maceo told him. "What you got planned? Tryin' to rob a bank or some shit?" he asked.

"Nah," Terrance answered. "Some lil' nigga tried to pull my hoe card earlier."

"Oh, word?" Maceo asked.

"Hell yeah. Some ole' Spanish lookin' curly haired mufucka," Terrance said.

Maceo nodded his head in understanding. "Well if you lookin' for somethin' simple to teach that fuck nigga a lesson, I suggest a semi-automatic. But," he said. "If you really tryin' to light some shit up I suggest a machine gun. And I got 'em for the low too," he told Terrance.

***

Terrance crept stealthily across Fiona's front lawn wearing a black ski mask and black attire from head to toe. Gripped tightly in his hands was a submachine gun.

Hassan and Fiona lay in the queen size bed peacefully and silent. As usual, Hassan was wide awake staring up at the popcorn ceiling while Fiona was fast asleep. He had actually gotten used to the sleepless nights.

Hassan slowly turned onto his side and stared at the dark bedroom wall. He was completely oblivious to the man outside looking to seek revenge.

Terrance quickly glanced at his surroundings. The entire neighborhood seemed to be on sleep mode. Quietly, he crept up the front steps. Once he reached the front door, he kicked the door inward causing it to fly off the hinges!

Hassan and Fiona instantly jumped up in bed at virtually the same time.

11

"What was that?" Fiona asked fearfully.

Hassan hurriedly snatched the sheets off and reached for his piece on the nightstand. Suddenly, the bedroom door swung open and Terrance immediately started spraying!

TAT! *TAT*! *TAT*! *TAT*! *TAT*! *TAT*! *TAT*! *TAT*! *TAT*!

Bullet's tore through the small dark bedroom one after the other. A bullet shattered the bedroom window while several impaled Fiona's body.

Hassan quickly dropped down onto the floor beside the bed and out of view, and cocked the Glock. His heart hammered rapidly in his chest as he lay on the floor.

"*Shit*!" he cursed to himself. This mothafucka had some balls after all!

Peering underneath the bed, he watched as Terrance's black Polo boots made their way towards him. With each step he took, Hassan's heart beat faster and harder.

Hassan acted fast as he reached up and let off several shots in Terrance's direction.

POP!

POP!

POP!

Hassan lifted his head up a little to see if he had hit his target—

TAT! *TAT*! *TAT*! *TAT*! *TAT*! *TAT*! *TAT*! *TAT*! *TAT*!

Terrance let off an entire clip in Hassan's direction. The shots lit the dark bedroom up as shells dropped onto the carpeted floor. Hassan lay flat on the floor, shielding his head. Fiona's queen size bed was the only thing in between both men. If Hassan was not lying on the floor beside the bed, his fate would have very well been the same as Fiona's.

More shells dropped onto the floor as Terrance continued to rain bullets in Hassan's direction.

Click! *Click*!

Terrance pulled the trigger, but unfortunately his machine gun was out of ammo. "Fuck!" he cursed.

Hassan quickly took advantage of this moment, and let off several shots in Terrance's direction. Unfortunately, he had no way of knowing if he had hit Terrance or not since he was shooting from on the ground and aiming the gun over the bed.

Terrance tossed the meaningless weapon on the floor, and darted out of the bedroom. He quickly ran through the hallway and jogged down the short flight of stairs. It wasn't until he reached the foot of the stairs that he realized he had been hit by one of Hassan's bullets.

Terrance reached down and touched the dime sized bullet wound on his abdomen. "Shit," he cursed in pain. He quickly made his way towards the front door, stumbling every few feet. He held onto the egg white walls for support. He was losing blood incredibly fast.

Meanwhile, upstairs, Hassan had finally mustered up enough courage to peel himself off the floor. His chest heaved up and down as he breathed heavily. He could not believe Terrance had come back full force on some vengeful type shit.

His eyes slowly wandered over towards the mattress where Fiona lay sprawled out in a pool of her own blood. A white blood stained sheet partially covered her nude body. Her eyes were wide open and glazed over.

"Fuck! Fuck! Fuck!" Hassan cursed tapping the butt of the gun against his head. "*Dammit*!"

In a sudden fit of rage, Hassan jumped off the mattress and raced downstairs. Terrance was already inside his car when Hassan burst through the front door. He quickly jumped from the porch and landed on the ground, slightly twisting his ankle in the process.

Terrance wasted no time as he started up the ignition to his car. He peered into the rear view window, and immediately noticed Hassan coming after him. Without hesitation, he jerked the gears into Drive and skirted off.

Hassan attempted to chase after the car even though his right ankle throbbed in agony. After realizing that it was no use chasing the car, he let off several shots.

POP!

POP!

POP!

POP!

One of the bullets shattered the back windshield of Terrance's Volkswagen, but it didn't deter him in the least as he quickly rounded the corner and disappeared.

"*Shit*!" Hassan cursed loudly.

He could not believe this shit had happened, and worst of all, he could not believe that he didn't prepare for it. Hassan knew how cutthroat Cleveland niggas could be. He should have been more on his shit. Hell, if he was maybe Fiona would still be alive.

"Damn!" he yelled.

The sudden sound of police sirens approaching let him know that he needed to flee the scene immediately.

***

"Let me hit that shit real quick," Maceo told his homie, AJ.

They were cruising through the hood, bumping French Montana's "*Ocho Cinco*", and blowing on some Grade A kush.

AJ passed him the tightly rolled blunt, and Maceo took an aggressive drag. As he inhaled the smoke, he continued to replay Terrance's words over and over in his mind.

Some ole' Spanish lookin' curly haired mufucka.

The more Maceo thought about the description, he realized how similar it sounded to Hassan. There were plenty of fellas who fit that particular description, but still he couldn't shake the thought that maybe...just maybe...Terrance was referring to Hassan...

***

Hassan slowly made his way up the cracked stone steps that led to the quaint little house he once called home. He had not stepped through the door of his house in over a week. The place that was once his residence now held far too many memories.

Parked directly across the street from Hassan's home was a suspicious black vehicle that if he had to guess was probably an officer surveying his home. They were probably hoping and expecting Nikki to show up at any minute. Hassan, however, didn't mind the officer watching his home. He knew Nikki would not be dumb enough to show up.

Hassan opened the front door and stepped into the home. The kitchen was the first room he entered. He took slow steps through the room. It was quiet. Unnaturally quiet. Living in a house with two other people, silence was something Hassan was not at all accustomed to.

Once he reached the refrigerator, he opened it to see if there was any beer. To his dismay, there was only a half empty can of Budweiser and a small box of two week old shrimp fried rice.

"Fuck," Hassan muttered under his breath. He desperately needed a drink or at least something to smoke to take his mind off the shit that had just happened.

Fiona was dead.

Some sheisty ass nigga was driving around in his car with over two million dollars in the trunk—if the guy had not already discovered it.

And Hassan was broke as hell.

"Fuck I'ma do?" Hassan asked himself closing the refrigerator.

The moment the refrigerator door closed, Hassan stared at the photos of him, Nikki, and Dre.

They each looked so happy, and worry-free…completely unaware of the events that would eventually tear them apart.

Hassan's gaze wandered towards Nikki's beautiful smile. *Damn that smile,* Hassan thought. An uncomfortable feeling settled in the pit of his stomach. He wanted to hate her so badly. He wanted to despise her for choosing Dre over him. After all it was hate that fueled his instincts to pull the trigger on her.

However, as Hassan stared at Nikki's picture on the refrigerator door, he couldn't deny the fact that he was still somewhat in love with her.

"Fuck," Hassan cursed. He ran his fingers through his curly hair. "Yo, what the fuck is wrong with me?" he asked himself.

Unable to stand the sight of Nikki any longer, he turned and walked away. As he walked past the kitchen counter, his fingertips glided across the laminate countertop. Hassan's mind may have been playing tricks on him, but the countertop still felt warm from when he and Nikki had made passionate love.

He shook his head. *I can't still be in love with a damn chick I tried to kill,* he thought to himself. *Can I*?

***

The following morning, Hassan awoke to the unexpected loud boom of the front door being kicked open. Before he had a chance to realize what was happening, several police officers rushed inside his bedroom with their guns drawn.

"Put your hands up and *slowly* get out of the bed!" one demanded.

It had been over a month since the US Marshalls had stormed into his home and arrested him due to being a possible accessory to robbery. Now the nightmare was recurring all over again.

"What did I do?" Hassan asked even though he had a pretty good idea about why they were there.

"Hassan Bashir, you have the right to remain silent. Anything you say can and will be held against you," a second officer began to read him the Miranda rights.

Another officer proceeded to cuff Hassan. He sighed in frustration. Could things possibly get any worse?

12

Maceo stepped into the dark motel room. The curtains were drawn, and it almost looked as if the room was vacant had it not have been for the small bundle underneath the covers and the television turned on.

Maceo placed the food he had brought onto the table, and made his way over to the curtains. After drawing them back, light immediately poured into the room.

The small bundle underneath the sheets slowly began to move around accompanied by soft groans. Seconds later, Nikki pulled the sheets from off her body, and shielded her eyes from bright light.

"Mornin'. Get ya ass up and put somethin' to eat in your stomach," Maceo said.

Nikki squinted as her eyes fought to adjust to the sunlight. "Mornin'," she greeted in a raspy tone. "And thanks."

Maceo handed Nikki a Styrofoam to go box and a 16 oz. Minute Maid orange juice. He then took a seat on the unused mattress across from Nikki and proceeded to eat his own breakfast.

Nikki opened the Styrofoam box. Inside was cinnamon French toast, scrambled eggs with cheese, two sausage links, and two bacon strips. Her tummy rumbled as she eyed the delectable food.

They ate in silence all up until the *39 Weeks of Pregnancy-March of Dimes* commercial came on TV. Nikki shuffled nervously in her seat, and tried to concentrate on eating.

"Do you and ya girl have kids?" Nikki suddenly blurted out. She immediately regretted asking the minute it came out. His personal life wasn't any of her concern. She was just grateful to have him in her corner.

Maceo surprised Nikki when he chuckled. Obviously he found her question amusing. "Nadia? And kids? Ha!" he said sarcastically. "I doubt that'll happen any time soon."

"Why's that?" Nikki asked. Her curiosity was getting the best of her.

Maceo released a sigh. "My uh...my girl...she obsesses of her own damn image. I mean, I guess she wasn't satisfied with her natural looks...so she went and got all these damn procedures done and shit," he explained. "Ain't no way in hell she's gonna wanna sacrifice her body to gimme a baby."

Nikki's eyebrows furrowed as she listened intently. "And are you really cool with that?" she asked.

Maceo forked the last of his eggs and ate it. He shrugged. "At first I was," he said. "But a nigga getting' older now. Hell, I'm pushing thirty. All that superficial shit ain't where it's at no more," he told Nikki. "And I'm damn sure tired of shelfin' money out to her ass so she could go and alter somethin' else about herself."

"Are you happy with her?" Nikki asked. She immediately regretted the question the moment it slipped from her lips. She was getting a little too personal. "I'm sorry," she quickly said. "You don't have to answer that."

Maceo wiped his hands. "You good," he reassured her. "I mean shit, you my home girl. I don't mind choppin' it up with you. But I—uh—I got mixed feeling about my own happiness," he told her. "Physically, yeah I'm a happy dude when it comes to Nadia. She got the body of a damn goddess. What nigga wouldn't be happy with that shit?" he asked. "But it's like, got damn...that's all the hell she got to offer now. She ain't stimulatin' my mind like I need my chick to do. Shit pussy is pussy. I can get that from anywhere. I need us to be here," he pointed from his eyes to Nikki. "You feel me?"

"Well, does she know how you feel?" Nikki asked.

Maceo pulled out a cigarette and lit the filter. "Nah. And I don't plan on tellin' her," he said. "She plays her part and a nigga can't really complain too much."

"But isn't that like settling?" Nikki asked. "Why would you settle for something other than what you really want?"

Maceo took a long pull on the cigarette and released the smoke. "Shit, we all settle for something in one form or another."

Nikki didn't respond as she continued to eat. Suddenly, an uncomfortable feeling settled in the pit of her stomach. She quickly clamped a hand over her mouth as vomit uncontrollably shot upward.

Nikki raced into the bathroom, and expelled her stomach contents into the toilet bowl. Maceo entered the bathroom soon after, took a seat on the edge of the bath, and rubbed Nikki's back as she vomited.

Once Nikki finally finished, she flushed the toilet and wiped her mouth with the back of her hand. Tiny beads of sweat rolled down her forehead. She felt exhausted and weak.

Maceo continued to rub her back. "You alright, ma?" he asked in a concerned tone.

"No," she said exasperatedly. "I'm pregnant..."

***

Hassan paced back and forth in the small, smelly holding cell. There was one window covered by mesh that was so small it could easily be overlooked. The room was lit only through unnatural light and offered little to no comfort to prisoners.

Positioned in the furthest corner of the room was a steel toilet, and a guy plopped on top of it taking a noisy, atrocious shit as if he were in the comforts of his own home.

This was Hassan's first time ever going to jail—even with the numerous robberies he had committed.

He didn't know what the police had in store for him. All he could think about was that his fingerprints were all over Fiona's house.

They're about to slap this murder charge on my ass, and I'll never see the light of the day, he thought. *Or my fucking money.*

Hassan continued to pace back and forth, and he contemplated his fate.

"*Aye*!" One of the prisoners barked. "Quit doin' that shit! It's gettin' on my mothafuckin' nerves!" he cursed.

Hassan stopped pacing long enough to survey the prisoner who had suddenly snapped on him. The guy was seated on the concrete slab that also doubled as an uncomfortable bed. There was clearly a look of irritation on his face.

The man appeared to be in his mid-thirties. His arms were folded across his chest, and he was visibly upset, however his frustration went beyond Hassan's excessive pacing. He had been charged with a DUI the night before, and he was already on probation. Unfortunately, this would be his third strike.

"My bad. I ain't think me mindin' *my* business would piss *you* off," Hassan said in a sarcastic tone. "Nigga, fuck you!"

The prisoner jumped up from his seat so quickly, you would have thought he was sitting on hot coal.

Without warning, he charged at Hassan full speed and began reigning blows down on his body.

One powerful punch after the other, the prisoner relinquished his anger on Hassan. In the process of fighting and scuffling, Hassan's black V-neck t-shirt was yanked over his head revealing his bare chest.

Initially, the inmate was giving it to Hassan, until Hassan quickly gained the upper hand. He flung the prisoner into the nearby brick and mortar wall causing the guy to run head first into.

The other inmates backed out of the way so that they wouldn't be struck, and the ones that were sleeping awakened quickly

Hassan viciously kneed and punched the shit out of his aggressor. The soles of their sneakers scraped against the tiled floor as they fought and maneuvered throughout the cell. Hassan slammed the inmate against the metal bars and proceeded to punch him in the face and head. The prisoner uncontrollably dropped onto his knees, but Hassan did not cease his assault.

Suddenly, several police officers rushed into the holding cell. "*Hey*!" a female officer shouted. "Break it up!"

Hassan did not stop his attack as he continued to rain blows on the worn out inmate. "Get yo' punk ass up!" he yelled. The prisoner was no longer fighting back. Evidently he had run out of energy and stamina. "Get yo' bitch ass up and fight, nigga!" Hassan barked.

"I said break it up!" the officer shouted again.

The inmate dropped limply onto the tiled floor, and Hassan prepared to kick him until the officers suddenly rushed and restrained him. He was then extracted from the cell while the other officers checked to see if the incapacitated inmate was still conscious.

***

There was an uncomfortable silence in the motel room as Nikki lay in the bed feeling somewhat still nauseous. She expected Maceo to up and leave—and even wondered if he wanted to, but was forcing himself to stay out of sheer sympathy. A part of her wished he would just leave, but a part of her was grateful that he had chosen to stay. She didn't want to be alone right now truthfully, as much as she hated to admit it.

"How far along are you?" Maceo asked in a low tone finally breaking the silence.

Nikki cleared her throat. "A little over a month," she whispered.

Maceo ran a large hand over his full, thick beard. "Damn," he sighed. "I—uh—Shit...I'm sorry—"

"I don't need you to be sorry for me," Nikki said coolly. "Nor do I need or want your pity about the situation. You don't even have to be here if you don't want to be," she told him. "You can leave..."

Maceo's jaw tensed. He stared at Nikki silently for several seconds. Even with the tough girl façade she put on, he could see right through her. "Do you?" he asked. "Do you *really* want me to leave?"

Nikki stared straight ahead at the paper towel commercial on TV. "I don't want you feelin' like you're obligated to look after me." She turned to look at Maceo. "Like I told you before, I appreciate everything you're doing for me...but I'm not some fuckin' charity case—and can you stop looking at me like that!" she snapped.

Maceo held his hands up defensively. "Like what?" he asked sarcastically.

"Like you feel sorry for me or some shit," she said.

Maceo snorted. "Damn. My fault, ma. It's just..." He walked over to Nikki's bed and took a seat. The mattress squeaked beneath his weight. "You act like its somethin' wrong with needin' somebody," he told her. "Everybody needs somebody at one point or another in their life."

Maceo was too close to Nikki for comfort. "Well, I don't nor have I ever needed anyone for anything," she said. "And I damn sure don't need you feelin' sorry for me."

Maceo started to respond until suddenly his cellphone began ringing.

Bands a make her dance.

Bands a make her dance.

All these chicks poppin' pussy, I'm just poppin' bands.

"What's up?" he greeted.

"Nigga, what's good?" AJ greeted boisterously. He was unintentionally on speaker phone since Maceo's cellphone was undergoing some technical issues.

"Shit, chillin' nigga. What's good?"

"You know that new spot Club Lush is havin' a grand openin' tomorrow night," AJ explained. "Everybody who's anybody is gon' be in that joint. The bitches gon' be deep. Nigga's gon' be poppin' bottles! What's up?" he asked. "You tryin' to slide through or what?"

Nikki's ears quickly perked up. Everybody who's anybody is going to be there. *Hmm*, she wondered if that was indeed the case.

"Yeah. That sounds cool," Maceo agreed. "We can slide through. I'ma hit you in a lil' bit."

"Aight dude," AJ said before disconnecting the call.

Maceo's gaze wandered back over towards Nikki. There was so much intensity in his dark eyes. He could both intimidate and turn a woman on with his powerful stare.

"I'm finna roll out then," he said. "Since you don't *need* me." He smirked and gave Nikki's leg a playful shove.

Nikki couldn't help but crack a slight smile. She regretted coming off so bitchy. It was a trait she could not help that she possessed. "I didn't mean...," she sighed. "I wasn't tryin' to come off...like *that*," she told him.

Maceo stood to his feet. "It's all good, baby girl," he told her. "You know that."

Nikki was totally taken back when Maceo kneeled over her and placed a soft peck on her forehead. Without another word, he left.

Staring at the motel door he had walked out of, Nikki slowly touched the spot on her forehead where he had just kissed her. She did not understand the gesture...but she would be lying to herself if she said she didn't like it.

13

Hassan was placed in a small individual holding cell that seemed damn near uninhabitable due to the miniscule space. The room was unnervingly quiet, and the only sound that could be perceived was the constant drips from the leaking faucet.

All alone, and with nothing to do, Hassan was stuck with his own thoughts. Thoughts that he had tried to push to the back of his mind with the help of alcohol, weed, and Black and Milds. He now knew that it was true what people said: one could literally go crazy in jail. His thoughts were consuming him, and nearly pushing him over the edge of sanity.

Every time he blinked, he saw Nikki's face. She was alive out there somewhere probably ready to hunt him down like a predator to its prey. What victim of betrayal wouldn't?

"How long are these mothafuckas gon' keep me in here?" Hassan asked himself. He was frustrated about even being there. He didn't pull the trigger on Fiona. He had definitely spilled his share of blood lately, but Fiona's was not on his hands.

BOOM!

Hassan punched the metal bars of the holding cell in a sudden fit of rage. He was so upset that he didn't even notice the large cut that had opened on his knuckles or the immediate swelling that followed soon after. His ankle was still a little sore from yesterday.

His plan was definitely not going accordingly.

***

The following morning, Nikki contemplated on the dangerous decision to go to the night club Lush's grand opening. If Maceo's friend was right about everybody who's anybody showing up then maybe—just maybe—she would see either Careem or Hassan. Or possibly both. She knew both men loved the party scene, especially Careem, and knowing Careem he could not pass up an opportunity to show off. He was far too obnoxious.

Like most people who came up on a hefty amount of cash, they would probably want to show it off, pop bottles, and brag, Nikki believed. There was the possibility, however, that both brothers could have possibly left the city, state, or even the country...but she hoped she could at least run into someone who might point her in the right direction. It was better to have some faith than none at all.

Maceo wanted her to stay in the confines of the boring motel room, but Nikki just couldn't do that. She would be damned if she sat back and let Dre's murder go unavenged.

***

A beautiful fair skinned nurse stepped inside Dre's hospital room. Long brunette hair flowed freely down her back, and stopped just inches above her round, firm ass. The on duty officer in Dre's room couldn't help but steal several glances at the attractive nurse when she wasn't paying attention.

I wish they would have made them like that when I was younger and single, he thought to himself. He was damn near salivating at the mouth, and disregarding the fact that he was a married man.

The nurse strutted over to Dre's hospital bed and prepared to inject him with his daily dose of medication. As usual, he was fast asleep—having not yet regained consciousness since his surgery—and hooked up to a heart-respiratory monitor.

Leaning slightly over his bed, she carefully lifted his left arm. The correction officer turned his head sideways in order to get a better angle of her ass.

Suddenly, and just as unexpectedly, Dre's eyes shot wide open immediately startling the nurse seconds before she stuck the needle inside his exposed vein. He grabbed her forearm aggressively, and quickly snatched the syringe out of her hand.

The nurse shrieked in fear, and the officer immediately reached for his weapon.

Dre quickly leapt out of the hospital bed, and roughly turned the nurse around so that her back was pressed firmly against his chest. He held the syringe against the side of her neck. The needle poked into her skin drawing a small amount of blood that slowly trickled down her neck.

"I'll kill this hoe, and not think twice about it," Dre said breathlessly. He felt extremely exhausted and tired. Apparently, lying in a bed for hours and hours consecutively could suck the energy out a person.

Tears slipped from the nurse's fearful eyes as she cried and plead with Dre to spare her. "Please," she begged. "Please don't kill me."

"Just let her go," the officer told Dre as he re-holstered his weapon. He then held his hands up defensively in order to give the impression that he was harmless. "Put the needle down nice and easy," he said in a calm tone. "You don't need any more trouble on your hands. Believe me."

"Fuck you!" Dre spat before forcefully shoving the nurse into him.

He then took off running out the room, and collided into a passing doctor causing his paperwork to fly up in the air. Dre quickly regained his footing and half-ran, half-walked down the hallway towards the nearest stairway.

He was extremely fatigued since he had not used his muscles in quite some time, and even lost his balance every few feet he ran. His heart hammered in his chest, and he had to hold onto the white sterile walls in order to keep his balance.

Dre's abdomen throbbed in pain from the surgery, but he continued to run ignoring the constant ache. He skipped down the flight of steps several at a time until he finally reached the main level.

Dressed in hospital attire, Dre raced through the main lobby instantly grabbing the attention of visitors, patients, and the hospital's security officers.

"*Hey*! Hey, stop!" one demanded.

Dre quickly leapt inside of the revolving door, and impatiently pressed against the glass to make it spin faster. Once outside, he took off running in the direction of oncoming traffic. He was too afraid to look over his shoulder to see how close the security officers were, but he knew without a doubt that they were pursuing him.

BEEP!

BEEP!

Drivers honked their horns, and tires burned the asphalt as they tried their hardest not to hit the deranged pedestrian running through traffic.

Dre ducked, dipped, and dodged several passing cars, and miraculously avoided two or three near accidents. He quickly came up on a white 2006 Honda Civic. Without thinking clearly—and with limited options—he yanked on the handle. To his surprise the door opened, and he anxiously jumped into the passenger seat.

A young, Puerto-Rican woman screamed in utter surprise and fear. Her five year old daughter instantly began crying in the backseat. The woman's automatic door locking system had been broken for an entire month, but unfortunately she did not have the money to repair it. She figured it would cause trouble sooner or later. Unfortunately, it was sooner than she had anticipated.

"What are you doing?!" she cried in fear.

Drivers honked their horns in irritation behind her.

"*Drive, bitch*!" Dre barked. He did not have a weapon on him to cause more fear in her, but he hoped his menacing tone was more than enough.

She quickly skirted off, fearful for her child's life as well as her own.

***

After an entire twenty-four hours of incarceration, Hassan was finally relinquished from custody.

Fingerprints had been lifted from the scene of Fiona's murder, evidence had been gathered up, and tests quickly proved that Hassan was not the triggerman after all. If that wasn't enough to aid in his case, Terrance had been arrested during his brief visit to the hospital, and quickly fingerprinted after intake. Hassan had once again managed to escape a lengthy imprisonment due to sheer luck.

Walking up Ontario Avenue, Hassan was freezing his ass off. A stretched out V-neck t-shirt, a pair of Levis, and no coat was definitely inappropriate attire for the cold weather. Downtown Cleveland was even colder than normal due to Lake Erie being only a hop, skip and jump away.

The walk to 6th street and West Huron was less than five minutes. Luckily he had enough change in his pockets to catch the RTA bus back home. The moment Hassan approached the bus stop shelter, he overhead two guys around his age talking about tonight's grand opening of some new night club called Lush.

Hassan's wheels immediately began to churn. He wondered if the mothafucka who had stolen his car would be there.

14

The sun had set hours ago, and Careem sat in the driver seat of his Maxima that was parked around the corner from Lush. He was bumping The Weeknd's "*Coming Down*" and in a hypnotic trance of his own as he stared down at the skinny line of cocaine on the back of his left hand.

Over the last few days he had taken heavily to the new drug. Usually, he was content with just blowing, but lately he needed something stronger. He needed something that would ease the emotional pain he fought so hard to deal with on a daily basis.

Leaning forward, he quickly sniffed up the small line of coke. It slowly made its way down his throat. He sighed deeply, and patiently waited for the high to come soon after. After all, being high was the only way Careem could tolerate living, dealing with himself, or even looking in the mirror for that matter.

The Weeknd's *Trilogy* CD changed to the next song which was *Loft Music*. Careem slowly felt himself slipping from the grip of sobriety. Reclining his head, he allowed the mellow tone of the music to stimulate him while the cocaine slowly worked its magic.

In the distance women chatted, and laughed as they made their way around the corner to the new club the entire city seemed to be talking about. Women were dressed in their best outfits, and wearing heels that seemed damn near impossible to walk in all for the mere love of attention.

Careem chuckled as he watched them, and shook his head. "Fuckin' city," he mumbled. After carefully dumping another small amount of cocaine onto the back of his hand, he quickly snorted it up his narrow nostrils.

***

I'm in my zone, I'm feelin' it.

Stop blowin' my buzz, quit killin' it.

So buy another round, they tried to shut us down...about an hour ago...

But we still in this bitch!

B.O.B.'s "*We Still in this Bitch*" played on maximum in the over-capacitated nightclub, and it was still fairly early.

Maceo, AJ, and a few of his other homies made their way through the thick crowd of people. Women gawked and smiled at Maceo as he passed them by barely giving the admirers a second look. He wasn't there to try to find the next chick he would climb up in, he just simply wanted to stunt.

Maceo looked fly as hell, and his swag was super heavy. Wearing a fitted black Givenchy t-shirt, his broad chest and buff, tattooed arms were on full display. A 14K white diamond tennis chain hung loosely around his neck complementing the diamond ring and iced out watch around his wrist. Designer jeans hung off his waist, and on his size fourteen feet were a pair of Giuseppe Zanotti sneakers. He was definitely dressed to impress for the occasion.

Several feet away, Nikki struggled to get through the crowd of people. Dressed in a black sweatshirt with the hood pulled low over her head, and a pair of black sweatpants, she looked more like an adolescent boy than an attractive woman. Of course, her attire's purpose was to shield her identity.

"Too many fuckin' people in here," she cursed to herself.

Nikki accidentally bumped into a guy as he was dancing, and sloshed some of the contents from his drink onto his plaid butt down shirt.

"Aye, lil nigga!" he sneered. "Watch it!"

Nikki ignored him as she continued to make her way through the crowd. She was strapped, and prepared for anything that may pop off.

***

Careem slowly made his way towards the bar, and took a seat in an empty bar stool. He was feeling nice much like he had hoped for. Now all he needed was a drink in his system.

A dark brown-skinned bartender made her way towards Careem. She looked a lot like singer, Kelly Rowland and even had the beautiful smile to match.

"What can I get for you baby?" she asked.

Careem's gaze wandered towards her cleavage spilling over the leather bustier she wore. "Shit," he licked his lips. "How about you?"

She flashed a cute dimpled smile. "All these girls in here," she said motioning towards the crowd. "Why don't you go get you one of them? There's plenty of them," she added.

Careem shrugged. "I don't want none of them," he told her. "I want you..."

"And I want to get your order so I can get back to my job," she retorted.

"So I see you gon' play hard to get," he smiled.

She shook her head, her curls shaking in the process. "Boy, you're too much for TV," she giggled.

Careem knew the *real* reason she wasn't interested. If he was still the *old* him, she would have gladly been on it. He had never had difficulty getting pussy. Especially easy pussy.

"Fuck it, let me get a double of Hen," he told her.

She turned around and walked off to fetch his drink, and he couldn't help but eye her tight, round ass in the dark skin tight jeans she wore.

Let me give a shout out to my real bitches.

Gon' bust it open for a real nigga.

French Montana's "*Shout Out*" blared through the club's massive speakers. Careem scanned the crowd. It was extremely packed; people were wall to wall, mingling, dancing, drinking, and having a good old fashion time.

No one knew or cared that he had almost been killed by his own brother. He had taken a bullet to the face, and lived to tell about it...but unfortunately his life would never be the same due to a physical defect.

Careem instantly tensed up just thinking about the horrific moment when Hassan had shot him, and left him for dead. Hell, Hassan had no idea that Careem was even still alive.

Suddenly, the beautiful brown skinned bartender returned and placed his drink in front of him. He slapped a crisp twenty dollar bill on the mahogany counter.

The bartender smiled, revealing that pretty set of dimples once more. "Is the rest my tip?" she asked with a flirtatious grin.

There was no hint of sarcasm in Careem's tone when he asked, "You gon' let me fuck?"

Her pretty face instantly transformed into a disgusted expression. "Not for no twelve dollars," she said with much attitude.

"Then bitch, bring me my change, and get the fuck out my face," he sneered.

"Fuckin' pig," she mumbled before walking off.

Even after cursing her out, he still watched her round ass switch in the hip hugging jeans.

***

Nikki continued to make her way through the crowd and towards the bar. She had ambled through the crowded dance floor, but it was far too many club goers to try to spot a specific person out.

"This was a waste of damn time even coming here," she told herself.

Asap Rocky's "*Fucking Problem*" played on maximum as she made her towards the bar. Suddenly, something caught her eye instantly stopping her in her tracks for several seconds. For a moment she even thought her eyes were playing tricks on her. *Could it be*, she asked herself. No…it can't be…

Careem sat on a barstool sipping on a drink completely oblivious to her presence. He wore a red Adidas hoodie, and a red and black Miami Heat snapback. Even with the stubble on his face, he was totally recognizable although she was only staring at a side profile of him.

Nikki quickly made her way over towards him with her hand on her piece. Maceo had given her a pistol for protection purposes only. Right about now she didn't give a fuck. She would blast his ass and not think twice about the setting or the number of witnesses.

Careem immediately noticed someone approaching him from his peripheral vision. He assumed it may have been one of his homies, or someone wanting to buy some green off him, but when he finally turned to see who it was, he nearly pissed himself.

The liquor slipped down his throat the wrong way, and he immediately went into a coughing fit. That, however, didn't stop him from taking off running in the opposite direction dropping his shot glass in the process. It immediately shattered upon impact.

Nikki took off running after him, bumping into and shoving people out of her way. She could not believe this motherfucker had the nerve to actually run from her. He was so pathetic that he couldn't even face her like a man. A 6'1 man running from a 5'2 woman. It couldn't get any sadder than that.

Careem pushed women and men out of his way as he ran full speed through the crowd. His hat flew off in the process, but he didn't dare think twice about retrieving it. Flashing strobe lights reflected off the people on the dance floor. Careem knocked drinks out of people's hands as he bolted past them, but he didn't give a damn about the threats they tossed at him afterward.

Nikki chased after him, making sure never to lose him from her sight. *I'm gonna kill this bastard,* she told herself repeatedly.

ASAP get like me.

Never met a motherfucker fresh like me.

All these motherfuckers wanna dress like me.

Put the chrome to your dome make you sweat like Keith.

Careem raced out of the dance floor area and into the narrow hallway that led to the restrooms. Nikki was hot on his heels!

"Whatchu' runnin' for?!" Nikki yelled after him.

"Fuck you bitch!" Careem yelled. "I should've let Hassan pop yo' hoe ass!" After his last remark, he quickly darted inside the men's restroom.

Nikki didn't give a damn about the hallway's cameras stationed in the upper corners of the ceiling. She drew her weapon and slowly made her way inside the men's restroom.

The moment, she placed a hand on the large white wooden door it swung outward slamming directly into her face! Before she had a chance to react, Careem literally snatched her inside the empty restroom and proceeded to strangle her!

The gun instantly dropped from her hand and landed onto the tiled bathroom floor. She could taste the bitter, salty taste of her own blood from when the door had slammed into her mouth.

Careem shook Nikki aggressively by her throat like a ragdoll, threatening to snap her slender neck at any given moment.

"I'ma kill ya lil' ass!" he screamed in rage.

Nikki's eyes were fastened to the restroom's ceiling as she fought to draw in air. She could slowly feel the life slipping out of her as he crushed her windpipe.

With limited options, Nikki quickly reached down, grabbed his testicles through his Camo cargo shorts, and squeezed.

"*Aaah*!" he cried out in pain before releasing her.

Nikki quickly dropped onto the dirty, urine stained tiled floor.

"You fuckin' lil' bitch!" Careem cursed.

Nikki quickly scrambled on her hands and knees towards the gun lying several feet away near the urinals. Before he could grab her, Nikki snatched the gun and aimed it directly at Careem. He froze in mid-movement, aware that if he took one more step she would start shooting without hesitation.

She quickly stood to her feet, and cocked the Glock. Suddenly, Nikki's facial expression changed from a hardened look to a softer, sympathetic expression. Her eyebrows furrowed in confusion as she stared at Careem's face.

Careem nodded his head in understanding. "Yep. You see this shit?" he asked her. "That mothafucka did this to me," he said in a calm tone.

Where his left eye used to be was a smooth, white globe. The conformer substituted as his eye, until his glass eye was manufactured.

"He did this shit to me!" Careem screamed. His loud voice echoed off the restroom's walls.

Nikki flinched at his unexpected tone. She then opened her mouth to say something, but quickly closed it after realizing she didn't exactly know what to say. Apparently, she was not the only person Hassan had double crossed.

Careem slowly outstretched his arms. "You wanna shoot me for the shit I did to you and Dre? That's what you wanna do, right?" he asked. "'Cause you wouldn't be here if you weren't." He held his arms out. "Go ahead," he told her. "Shoot me. Pull the fuckin' trigger. Put me out of my fuckin' depressin' ass misery." He laughed sadistically, but in his eye there was no trace of humor whatsoever.

Nikki did not budge. She simply stood there with a confused expression on her face, unable to seek the revenge she desperately wanted to deliver.

"Do it!" Careem barked.

Nikki flinched again. The gun trembled slightly in her small hands.

Suddenly Careem walked over towards Nikki, grabbed her hands which were wrapped firmly around the gun, and held them at his own head.

"Did you hear me?" he asked. "I said kill me. Shoot me. Pull the damn trigger." He stared deep into Nikki's eyes and she stared back unblinkingly.

15

It was obvious Careem had a death wish. Just minutes ago Nikki was hell bent on ending his life, but now that the moment had come, she could not even pull the fucking trigger.

"Kill me!" Careem barked. He pressed his forehead against the barrel of the gun. "Did you hear me you dumb bitch?! I said kill me! *Kill me*! *Shoot me*! Pull the fuckin' trigger already!" Spittle flew from his mouth as he shouted. "KILL ME!"

"*Nooooo*!" Nikki cried slowly lowering her weapon. Tears spilled over her lower lids. "I...I can't...," she finally admitted.

Careem stared down at Nikki in disgust, and shook his head. "You're a weak bitch," he told her. "You and Hassan really *did* belong together."

Nikki looked down at the dirty tile beneath her feet. She could not even meet his gaze after that remark.

"Ya'll mothafuckas cut from the same cloth," he said.

Without another word, Careem slowly exited the men's restroom.

***

Hassan quickly made his way across the parking lot towards a young Puerto-Rican guy flirting with a cute black female. They were both leaning against the trunk of a red sports car, totally unaware of the mysterious stranger approaching them.

Hassan had one arm behind his back as he walked up on the two of them. Clutched tightly in his hand was a rusty lead pipe he had found on the ground. Since he was not strapped he had to take a different approach to get his point across, however, he did not mind being creative.

Hassan recognized the guy almost immediately, but spotted the car way before he even saw him. The factory rims had been removed—and probably sold—and now the car sat on four donuts. There were not too many guys in Cleveland whipping custom Ferraris so Hassan knew without a doubt it was Careem's. The entire purpose for him coming to the club was because he had hoped to run into the guy who had stolen his car, and fortunately he had "lucked up". Niggas couldn't resist the temptation to stunt and show off during the grand opening of a new club.

Hassan could not believe his eyes as he watched the red Ferrari pull into the parking lot of Club Lush several minutes earlier. He stayed out of view and waited until the perfect opportunity to strike.

The young Puerto-Rican guy was having too much fun flirting with the female in the parking lot that he wasn't even concerned with checking out the new night club. She had his undivided attention.

"So I'm sayin' though, mami, why don't you just slide with me, and we can go somewhere and kick it," he suggested. "Just you and me."

She smiled and twirled a tendril of hair. "You know I came with my girls," she said. "And I don't even know your name yet..." She offered a flirtatious grin.

"Frisco," he told her. "My name's Frisco. So now that you know my name, what's up, mami?" he asked putting on a charming smile. "You tryin' to roll out with ya boy?"

She shrugged, grinning. "I still don't know..."

Frisco was just about to respond, before Hassan suddenly spoke up. "Aye! I been lookin' all over the city for ya mothafuckin' ass!" He shouted from several feet away.

Frisco and the female turned in Hassan's direction as he approached them. They didn't even see or hear him approaching until he finally made his presence known. The entire parking lot was empty besides the three of them, and the entrance to the club was around the corner so there wasn't another person in sight.

Frisco made a face in disgust. "Who the fuck are you?!" he asked.

"I'm that nigga you shouldn't have fucked with!"

WHAP!

Hassan suddenly smashed lead pipe down onto Frisco's skull. He dropped onto the ground instantly.

Frisco's new female friend shrieked and backed away. "Oh my God!"

"Fuck outta here," Hassan told her.

She did not have to be told twice as she quickly took off running. Her blue platform pumps clicked against the asphalt.

"What the fuck man?!" Frisco cried clutching the back of his head. Blood gushed out of a small, deep cut that had opened. He then looked at his hand which was now covered in thick red blood. "Que diablos? What the fuck is your problem, man?!"

Hassan reached down and grabbed Frisco by the collar of his shirt, snatched him up, and slammed him against the sports car. "Nigga, you thought I really wasn't gon' find ya punk ass?" he asked pointing the lead pipe in Frisco's face.

"Come on man," Frisco cried. He was drooling like a damn new born baby, afraid for his life. He had never thought about the consequences he could possibly face after stealing the car. All he saw were dollar signs. "Look, it wasn't nothin' personal," he said. "You know how it is out here. I'm just tryin' to do what I gotta do to eat. You feel me?"

Hassan snorted, clearly offended by Frisco's lame ass apology. "Do I feel you?" he repeated sarcastically. "*Nigga, feel this*!"

WHAP! WHAP!

Hassan smacked Frisco in the face twice with the lead pipe!

Frisco went crashing down onto the asphalt. He spat out several teeth, and a mouthful of dark red blood.

Hassan stared down at Frisco who was now on his hands and knees struggling to stand up and coughing up blood. Every time he tried to stand, he fell back onto the ground. His head spun, and throbbed in pain from the vicious blows.

Suddenly, and without warning, Hassan kicked Frisco in the ribs.

"*Aaarrggh*!" he cried in pain, falling over onto his side. He then cradled his injured chest. "Come on man…I'm sorry! Please don't kill me man!"

"Shut that shit up," Hassan told him emotionlessly. Satisfied with the damage he had caused, Hassan turned towards the car. He looked around briefly, and then turned towards Frisco. "Where's the mothafuckin' keys at?!" he barked.

Still clutching his ribs, Frisco slowly pulled the keys from his back pocket, and tossed them at Hassan's feet. "There! Take it! It's yours! Just please don't kill me man."

Hassan knelt down, and retrieved the car keys. While bending down, he peered at the license plates on the back of the car. It had been replaced with a new—probably fabricated— one.

He looked over at Frisco in disgust and kicked his Nike shoes aggressively. "You real foul nigga," Hassan said.

Turning his attention back to the vehicle, he proceeded to unlock the trunk—he suddenly, noticed there was a small dent on the trunk. The dent was small, but it was obviously major enough because the trunk refused to open.

"This bitch jammed! What the fuck?!" Hassan yelled in irritation.

Soft thunder roared in the sky, and tiny rain drops began to fall to the earth.

He turned towards Frisco. "What's in the mothafuckin' trunk?!" he yelled.

"I don't know," Frisco cried. Blood seeped out of his mouth. "I never went in it—"

Hassan kicked Frisco's leg. "Don't lie to me mothafucka!"

"I swear on my grave—"

"Nigga, you gon' be swearin' on ya grave, aight," Hassan threatened.

"I never opened the trunk. I backed into a pole the night I stole it. I was drunk as fuck, man. I never went in it, I swear!" Frisco cried!

Hassan tossed the keys at Frisco in a fit of rage. "I should kill your bitch ass!" he said.

"Please," Frisco cried. "Come on bro'. You got your car. Please let me live. I'm not even worth it dude. Look at me." He shook his head, and grinned revealing a bloody toothless smile. "I ain't shit," he cried. "Just let me go..."

Hassan actually felt sorry for this chump. He had been intent on putting a bullet in Frisco's head ever since he had stolen his car, but decided against killing him." I'm givin' ya ass three seconds to get the fuck outta here!"

Frisco quickly scrambled to his feet, and ran off grateful that his life had been spared.

Hassan shook his head and slowly rounded the car. After opening the back door, he pulled the latch that folded the backseat. He wondered why Frisco had not thought to do this, but figured it probably hadn't crossed his mind.

To Hassan's amazement, the duffle bag was still in the trunk. He quickly retrieved it, happy to feel that the weight of it was still the same.

"Hell yeah," he smiled to himself. "That's what the fuck I'm talkin' 'bout."

Hassan closed the back door—the sudden sound of a gun being cocked stopped him dead in his tracks...

16

Hassan slowly turned around to face the person who was obviously armed. His first thought was that it had to be Frisco. *I knew I should have killed that nigga,* he thought to himself.

The moment Hassan locked gazes with the last person he expected to see, he suddenly froze in place. Less than three few away, Nikki stood with her gun aimed directly at him. The hoodie to the sweatshirt she wore was pulled low over her head, and the look in her beautiful eyes was one of pure anger and vengeance.

Hassan snorted and shook his head in utter disbelief. *You got to be fucking kidding me,* he thought to himself. The timing couldn't have been any damn worse. It seemed like every time he got his hands on the money some crazy shit always seemed to happen. It all started with Careem pulling the gun on him.

Hassan held his hands out and gave Nikki an expression that said 'so are you going to shoot me or not?'

Nikki's grip on the gun was firm as she stared into Hassan's cold eyes. The tiny raindrops quickly turned into heavy ones as thunder roared above.

Hassan spoke first. "So whatchu gon' do, Nikita?" he asked referring to her real name. "You gon' stand there...or you gon' shoot me...?"

Nikki's nostrils flared in anger. Tears pooled in her eyes. She had dreamt about this moment, and it was pure intuition that even led her to the parking lot to begin with, but now that she was finally face to face with the man who had betrayed her she was having difficulty pulling the trigger.

Nikki had even contemplated on going to their old house to look for him, and hopefully put a bullet in his head as he slept, but she figured he wouldn't be dumb enough to go home. That would be far too easy. She also was not bold enough to go somewhere where she knew was under heavy surveillance.

Hassan nodded his head in understanding. "It's about the money ain't it?" he asked with a serious expression. "Here..." he dumped half of the contents from the duffel out. Stacks of money plummeted to the wet ground.

"It's not about the fucking money, Hassan," Nikki said through gritted teeth. Tears streamed down her cheeks, and she did not bother wiping them away. "We were friends—no we were *family*!"

"Family?!" Hassan repeated in a sarcastic tone. "You and Dre were family. A perfect fuckin' family. Remember that? It was always just about ya'll. I been sticking my neck out, and puttin' my life on the line for ya'll mothafuckas all my life...so why get salty when I finally decide to look out for me—"

"I would've never done you like that Hassan! I would've never hurt you—"

"Well what the fuck do you call what you did to me?!" he yelled.

Nikki's bottom lip trembled as she fought to contain herself from crying hysterically. To be honest, she had never taken Hassan's feelings into serious consideration. "I was hurt too, Hassan," she admitted in a low tone.

"Bullshit!" Hassan yelled. "You weren't hurt. You ain't give a fuck," he told her. "All you thought about was ya damn self." He pointed to his chest. "So I finally had to think about myself. Don't hate on a nigga for doin' that," he said coldheartedly. "'Cause real talk...we're two of a kind."

Nikki replayed Careem's words over in her mind. Shaking her head, she whispered. "No. We're nothing alike, Hassan."

"We are," he told her. "We are and you know it."

The gun trembled in her hand as she kept it aimed at Hassan. The rain poured heavily from above, but unfortunately it could not wash away the pain and betrayal she felt.

"I would have never pulled a gun out on you, Hassan," she admitted.

He began to take slow steps towards her. "*That,*" he began. "Was the only thing I regretted doing when all that shit popped off," Hassan told her. "I guess...I was just so fuckin' mad at your ass. You told me that if the baby was mine, you'd let this nigga raise it. What type of shit is that, Nikki?" he asked.

Nikki didn't respond as she stared into Hassan's light brown eyes.

"I hated your mothafuckin' ass after you said that shit," he confessed. "You hurt me so damn bad, Nik. I...I wanted to hurt you too somehow..."

Hassan was so close to Nikki that the barrel of her gun was pressed firmly against his chest.

"I hated you too," Nikki finally admitted. "You knew about Dre and Adorable. You knew that I was hurt that night and you still took advantage of me," she told him. "Damn, I loved you too though. Dre was my man but you, Hassan you were supposed to be more than that."

Hassan was obviously still hurting inside. The beast inside of him had been released during the day of the robbery, but now that he was face to face with Nikki he seemingly returned to his old self. "I was caught in the middle," he said. "Dre was my dude too. It's hard to pick sides. And what difference would it have made anyway? Huh?" he asked. You still picked him after what the fuck he did. Pull the trigger, take the money, or put the gun down..."

Hassan and Nikki stared into one another's eyes unblinkingly. Hassan slowly lifted his hand, placed it on the barrel of the gun and gradually lowered it.

Surprisingly, Nikki allowed him to do this without a word or hint of hesitation. Slowly, Hassan eased the gun out of Nikki's hand. Tears streamed down her cheeks as she lowered her head towards the wet ground. Her chest heaved as she took deep breaths. The rain got heavier as her heart rate increased.

Hassan held her gun loosely in his hand as they stood inches apart from each other. Instead of looking her old friend in the eyes, she was instead staring at the ground. Careem's words continued to haunt her...

You're a weak bitch.

As Hassan stood in front of Nikki holding on to her gun, she thought about the possibility of him pulling the trigger on her for the second time...

17

Hassan slowly stepped around Nikki. She stood completely still as he walked around her. She assumed that he could not look in her the eyes when he shot her so instead preferred to face her back.

Nikki silently chastised herself for allowing him to take the weapon from her, but she honestly didn't have it in her to pull the trigger.

Nikki closed her eyes and suddenly felt the warmth of Hassan's body against hers. His hands slowly lowered around her bruised neck, and initially she didn't know what exactly he was about to do.

He unexpectedly placed a diamond flower necklace around her neck. It cost nearly four thousand dollars and once belonged to Timothy's older sister before her untimely death. The gesture was a subtle attempt at apologizing since he couldn't come right out and say it. After all, how exactly could you apologize after trying to take a person's life?

He then placed a palm against her flat belly from behind. Tears continued to run down Nikki's cheeks. The moment was a mixture of tenderness, confusion, hatred, and love.

Without another word, Hassan turned and walked off into the night. For several seconds, Nikki simply stood in place staring at nothing in particular. Suddenly, she burst into a fit of hysterical cries.

This is all so fucked up, she kept telling herself. *None of this shit was supposed to happen.* What hurt most of all was that things would never return to the way they used to be.

Nikki's tear-filled gaze then wandered over towards the drenched stacks of money on the ground less than several feet from where she stood.

***

Dre puffed on a Marlboro massaging his temples as he sat in a floral print recliner. He had smoked an entire pack of cigarettes in half a day; his nerves were on edge, and he had no idea what his next move would be. He was flat broke, wanted, and to make matters worse, he was now harboring hostages.

Lola Hernández held her sleeping daughter in her arms, as she stared intently at Dre from the sofa. Her expression was a combination of irritation and fear. For several hours she was forced to deal with Dre's presence. After hopping in her car, he had demanded that she take him to her home since it was the one place he felt was safe and secure.

"How much longer are you going to be here?" Lola finally worked up enough courage to ask.

Dre exhaled smoke through his nostrils. "You ain't in the position right now to be askin' mothafuckin' questions," he said in a calm tone.

Lola's eyes lowered to the tan shag carpet.

Dre's attitude softened as he stared at Lola for what felt like the first time. She was actually a very attractive woman. Her golden bronze skin was smooth and blemish free. Long, dark burgundy hair hung just inches from her waist. It was wavy from having washed it earlier and allowing it to air dry. Lola's emerald eyes were complimented by long, thick eyelashes, and a Marilyn Monroe-like beauty mark was positioned above her full, thick lips.

"I didn't mean to call you a bitch earlier," Dre confessed. "What's your name...?"

Lola's emerald eyed gaze lifted from the carpet to Dre. "Lola," she mumbled. "Is it okay if I tuck my daughter in?" she asked.

Dre took another pull on the cigarette, released the smoke through slightly parted lips, and smashed the filter into the glass ashtray on the coffee table. "Don't try any funny shit, Lola," he said without looking at her.

Lola slowly stood from the sofa, carrying her sleeping daughter in her arms. Dre watched as she departed from the living room.

Lola carried her daughter towards her small bedroom located at the end of the hallway. Once inside the bedroom, she softly laid Nina in her fairytale princess canopy bed. Nina stirred softly.

"Ssshh, ssshh," Lola said in a soft tone. She then pulled the covers over her daughter and planted a kiss on her forehead.

Standing to her feet, she quietly made her way out the bedroom. Once in the hallway, she slipped her Samsung cellphone from her back pocket, and punched in the digits 9-1-1.

Lola peered over her shoulder to make sure Dre was not around.

"Nine-one-one emergency. How may I help you?" a female dispatcher asked.

"There's a man in my home," Lola whispered. "He's holding me and my daughter hostage—you have to come quick," she said in a low tone.

"Ma'am, please provide your address."

"Two—"

Suddenly, a hand reached out and snatched the cellphone from Lola! Dre broke the flip phone into two pieces. She stared up at him in fear expecting him to strike her at any given moment.

"Next time it'll be me breakin' my foot off in ya ass," he threatened. Dre had to put fear in Lola's heart so that she would know he wasn't fucking around.

***

Maceo tossed the butt of the cigarette onto the wet ground and slowly made his way towards Nikki's motel room. It was a little past midnight. He didn't stay at Lush for too long due to a fight that had broken out. The police came and nearly pepper sprayed the entire club. Everyone ran out of Lush in a state of panic coughing and wheezing. One could never have a decent night without some crazy shit popping off.

Cleveland nightlife, Maceo thought to himself.

After sticking the keycard inside the door, he pushed it open. Nikki was on his mind, and he wanted to check up on her. There was only one lamp turned on. She lay in the center of the bed with her back turned to him.

Her soft sniffles let him know that something was obviously wrong. “Nikki? You good ma?” he asked.

Nikki didn’t respond as she continued to keep her back turned to him. Tears streamed from her eyes as she stared at the light gray wall. Her mind was totally in shambles. The one opportunity she had to seek revenge against Hassan had slipped through her fingers. Everything she had gone through to find him had all been for nothing.

Nikki felt hurt, confused, and much like she had betrayed her own self. She thought that once she confronted Hassan, the pain would go away, but it didn’t and she was still in the same exact situation. A pregnant wanted fugitive who was all alone in this cruel world and not even the four hundred thousand dollars stuffed in a shopping bag under her bed could change that fact.

Maceo slowly made his way towards Nikki’s bed. He took a seat on the edge of the bed. The mattress creaked upon his weight. “You aight?” he asked in a concerned tone.

Nikki wiped her tears, but didn't respond.

Maceo was not the best when it came to consoling. He was a street nigga who was only affiliated with other street niggas. Even the females he messed with were hard ass. He wasn't used to rubbing backs while promising everything would bc okay.

Not knowing what exactly to do or say to comfort his friend, he lay down in the bed and held her close. His strong arm rested on her tiny waist. Nikki was so small compared to his massive height.

As Dre's homeboy held Nikki close to his body, she couldn't help but feel comfortable and safe in his embrace.

18

Sunlight poured into Nikki's motel room as she cracked her eyelids open. She slowly turned and looked over her shoulder. Maceo lay in the same position as he had fallen asleep. His arm was draped casually over her waist as if they were longtime lovers. She felt so secure and protected lying next to him.

Nikki knew she shouldn't feel the way she did, but she could not help it. She stared at Maceo for several seconds as he slept soundlessly. His arm suddenly tightened around her waist, and he scooted her closer to him.

Nikki slowly closed her eyes and drifted back to sleep. As the two friends slept peacefully in the same bed, they were completely unaware of Maceo's cell phone vibrating on the nightstand. Nadia's cellphone number flashed across his screen. As expected, she wanted to know where the hell her man was.

***

Dre puffed on a cigarette at the wooden kitchen table, and watched as Lola cooked breakfast. She scrambled the eggs aggressively in the nonstick skillet. She hadn't cooked with this much attitude since her nothing ass baby daddy used to live with her. Lola was tired of Dre smoking up all her cigarettes, and living in her house much like he belonged.

She had missed work today, and Nina had been deprived of going to school. It was crazy how a person's life could be turned upside down in the blink of an eye. She didn't ask for any of this. Lola was simply at the right place at the wrong time.

After placing the scrambled eggs on a porcelain plate next to two strips of bacon, and toast, she brought the food over to Dre and slammed it down in front of him.

A piece of bacon fell from the plate and landed onto the table. Dre looked up at Lola, but she didn't care that he could sense her attitude. She was pissed off, and wanted to get back to her normal life.

Dre picked the bacon up and bit into it.

Lola stood in front of the table, and watched him eat with a disgusted look on her pretty face. She folded her arms underneath her breasts. "How long are you going to keep us?" she asked in an irritated tone. "People are going to start getting suspicious when I don't show up to work and Nina doesn't show up to kindergarten.

Dre stuffed a mouthful of eggs inside his mouth. He had not thought about that possibility. Instead he was too busy thinking about what the hell he was going to do. He had no money, Nikki was dead, and he had no idea how he was going to get out of the country.

"I'll let you go back to work and your daughter back to school tomorrow," Dre told Lola. "But then after that you have to come right back home."

Lola looked relieved.

Dre wasn't a fool however. "Just know I know niggas that know niggas, and if you try some funny shit...please believe you gon' regret it," Dre threatened.

***

"And double bag my shit this time," Careem said. "Last time I dropped an entire fuckin' six pack in the driveway of my crib."

The cashier scowled at Careem as he double bagged his bottle of liquor. "Have a good day," he said in a flat tone.

Careem took the bag, and walked out of the store. Once he reached his vehicle, he placed the bag on the hood of the car, and proceeded to unlock the door—suddenly, a pair of large hands wrapped a brown sack around Careem's head from behind.

The car keys dropped from his hands instantly as he desperately tried to defend himself. He was however no match against the large bodyguard that was now dragging him towards the nearby 2011 Cadillac Escalade.

"*Geerrrroff meee*!" Careem shouted in a muffled voice as he kicked and thrashed about helplessly. The soles of his vintage Adidas scraped against the pavement as he was forcefully dragged across the parking lot.

The bodyguard roughly tossed Careem into the backseat of the Escalade, climbed in and slammed the door behind himself. In the SUV were three other mysterious men. A second bulky body guard in the backseat, and a driver in the front.

Lexer turned slightly in the passenger seat, puffed on a Goldwin Louixs cigar, and eyed Careem through squinted yellow tinted eyes.

***

Wearing a brown sack over his head with both his arms tied in front of him with a self-locking cable tie, Careem was totally defenseless.

He had been snatched out of the truck seconds ago and was now walking through some unknown setting. The body guard behind him shoved Careem forcefully. He accidentally tripped and fell uncontrollably onto the cracked concrete.

"Get his ass up," a deep, baritone voice demanded.

Careem was forcefully grabbed off the ground and helped upright so that he kneeled on his knees. The brown sack was then yanked off his head.

Careem anxiously took in his surroundings. He was in the center of a junkyard, and had no idea what the intentions of the four men surrounding him were.

"The fuck is this?" Careem asked fearfully. His eyes darted from one man to the next. "Why I am here? The fuck ya'll want?!"

Lexer slowly made his way over towards Careem. He used an adjustable white support cane to aid him with his steps. A birth defect had forced him to use one all his life.

"It wasn't hard finding you," Lexer said nonchalantly. "You run your mouth *entirely* too much, Mr. Bashir."

"What the hell is this shit?!" Careem asked again.

"You, along, with several friends robbed a man recently," Lexer began. "That man, Timothy Baxter, was a client of mine. A client that had yet to pay back the money I was entitled to—"

"This shit is about that fuckin' robbery?!" Careem asked in disbelief. "Man, fuck that nigga and fuck you!" he yelled. "I ain't get to spend a dime of that money! The fuck this shit got to do with me?!"

Lexer sighed in frustration and tossed one of his body guards a look. A look that did not need to be accompanied with words.

Suddenly, a massive fist was brought down onto the back of Careem's head! He fell back down onto the ground only to be stomped and kicked by the two stocky bodyguards. One forceful blow cracked two of his ribs. Careem spit up a mouthful of blood as he was brutally kicked and stomped.

They would have killed Careem if it had not been for Lexer holding up his hand to signal for them to stop their attack.

Careem coughed and choked on his blood as he bled internally. He gasped for air, and gripped his injured ribs. "*Aaahhh*!" he cried in pain.

"Pick his ass up," Lexer said in a cool tone.

One of the body guards lifted Careem up so that he stood on his feet. His legs were weak beneath him, and he was unable to stand on his own. Both bodyguards held him by his arms, as Careem slowly felt himself on the verge of losing consciousness.

Lexer slowly approached Careem and stood face to face with him. He was so close that their noses were only inches from touching one another. "I am not going to play games with you," Lexer said. "I'm not one of your little *homies* in the street, or one of your little clients you sell that trash ass weed too. Oh yes," Lexer said. "I know about you. We can be here for hours doing this shit the hard way until you tell me what I need to know. I am an *extremely* creative man, Mr. Bashir. By the time I'm done with you, you'll be begging me to kill you."

Careem's eyelids fluttered as he fought to remain conscious. Thick dark red blood dripped off his chin.

Lexer grabbed a handful of Careem's hair and pulled his head back so that he could get a good look at his face. He wanted Careem to know that he was not fucking around. "Tell me where I can find Nikita Brown…"

Careem's chest heaved up and down as he took shortened breaths. His entire body ached in pain. He knew before it was all said and done, Lexer would kill him regardless. "Fuck you," Careem said before spitting a mouthful of blood into Lexer's face.

For several seconds, Lexer simply stood there. He did not react immediately. As a matter of fact, he did not seem to be phased by the disrespectful act.

Careem cracked a malicious smirk showcasing his bloodstained teeth. "Fuck you, you ugly mothafucka," he said before cackling hysterically.

Lexer released his hold on Careem's hair, and slowly stepped away from him. Suddenly, and without warning, Lexer snatched the gun out that had been tucked in his dress pants.

POP!

He fired a single shot that landed in Careem's left kneecap!

"*AAAHHH*!" Careem bellowed. Instinctively, he gripped his knee which was now gushing blood uncontrollably. "*Fuck*!" Pain tore through his entire body after the gunshot.

"We can do this the easy way or the hard way," Lexer told Careem.

"Fuck you!" Careem spat. "Fuck you mothafucka!"

The bodyguards could not believe Careem's resilience.

Lexer remained calm as he slowly made his way over towards Careem, the gun hung loosely at his side.

Careem's eyes were filled with fear, but he was not about to beg for his life. He didn't with Hassan and he wasn't about to with Lexer.

Lexer slowly aimed the gun at Careem's skull.

"You gon' kill me?" Careem asked. "Go ahead—pull the fuckin' trigger! I don't give a fuck! Shoot me!"

Lexer cracked a smile. "Well you see, Mr. Bashir," he said. "That'd be the easy way." Suddenly, and just as unexpectedly, he snatched out Careem's conformer.

"Aaaah! Shit!" Careem cursed reaching for where his left eye used to be.

Lexer dropped the smooth, white globe onto the cracked concrete and stepped onto it.

"Put his ass in the trunk," Lexer told his bodyguards.

A look of panic suddenly swept over Careem's face. "No!" he yelled. "*NO*!"

Both bodyguards dragged him to the nearest junk car. The trunk was already propped open.

Careem stared at his fate. "NO!" he cried. "*Get the fuck off me*!"

His tennis shoes scraped against the concrete as he was forcefully dragged to the rusty, broken down 1976 Cadillac Fleetwood.

Careem was all but crammed inside the tiny trunk. "*You mothaf—*"

His curses were cut short as the trunk slammed shut.

Lexer relit his Louixs cigar as he watched his bodyguards douse the vehicle with gasoline. He took several puffs on the expensive cigar and slowly made his way over towards the Cadillac.

Careem pounded his fist against the roof of the truck and shouted out obscenities.

Lexer took a final puff on his cigar before tossing it into the puddle of gasoline near the car. The Cadillac ignited in flames seconds later.

"We're done here," Lexer said.

19

Maceo and Nadia were at a table in the popular restaurant Zanzibar located in Shaker Heights. Although Maceo could get quite caught up in his hustle and the street life, he always tried to make quality time for his lady.

Seated across from him, sipping on a glass of red wine, Nadia looked absolutely breathtaking. She wore a Fina Ponte peplum mini dress, and on her pedicured feet were a pair of Christian Louboutin Zoulou leather platform sandals. A diamond necklace and chain complemented her attire. As always she was the baddest chick wherever she went...but Maceo barely seemed to notice her.

Instead his mind was elsewhere...specifically on a female that had no business being on his mind.

Maceo and Nadia's waitress returned with her notepad out ready to take their orders. "Have you two made up your mind yet on what you wanna order?" she asked cheerfully.

Nadia glanced down at her menu. "I'll have the garden salad, please," she ordered.

The waitress then turned her attention to Maceo who was still daydreaming. "And what can I get for you sir," she asked.

Maceo didn't respond. As a matter of fact, he didn't even notice the waitress's presence. He was too busy reminiscing about how good Nikki felt in his arms. *Why can't I get this damn chick off my mind,* he kept asking himself. Nikki wasn't even the type of female Maceo went for. She was too damn stubborn and hardheaded. He liked his women cooperative and submissive. But there was something about her...Every time he stared into her beautiful slanted hazel eyes she did something unexplainable to him. His stomach would churn and get butterflies like he was a damn little ass kid back in elementary school. No woman had ever had that effect on him.

I shouldn't even be thinking about my dead homie's pregnant girl like that, he kept telling himself. However, every time he tried to shake Nikki from his thoughts she always seemed to weasel her way back in—

"Maceo?" Nadia called out in irritation. She snapped her fingers to break him from his train of thought. "The waitress is talking to you."

Maceo cleared his throat and sat up in his seat. "Uh...let me get that catfish dinner," he said.

"What two sides would you like?" she asked. "We have yams, macaroni and cheese, French fries, coleslaw—"

"Let me get that yams and coleslaw," he ordered.

The waitress scribbled the orders down on a notepad, and beamed. "I'll put that in right away," she said before walking off.

Nadia gave Maceo a concerned expression. "Are you alright, baby?" she asked. "You've been kinda out of it lately," she told him.

Maceo wet his thick lips. "I'm straight," he assured her.

Nadia took another tiny sip from her red wine. "Oh, baby, I didn't even tell you about the fight I almost got into at work," she said. "Chick was mad 'cause I went up on stage during her turn. I mean, the DJ was calling her name for like five minutes and she didn't show up. I think the bitch was upstairs in the VIP turning tricks. Anyway, there can be no more than a two minute gap between each performance on stage so I took my happy ass up there. She tried to confront me in the locker room...."

Nadia's voice trailed off as Maceo tuned her out. His mind had uncontrollably drifted back to Nikki.

"Maceo, you're not even listening to me," Nadia whined.

Maceo's attention refocused on his woman. He lied and said, "I was listening to you, bay." He placed a hand over hers for reassurance.

Nadia smiled. "You haven't forgot about my birthday next week?" she asked giddily.

Damn. *I forgot all about her birthday*, he thought to himself. "Of course not," he lied.

Nadia looked pleased that her man had not forgotten about her special day. "So," she began. "I guess now that I got you here, I should ask where were you last night? I was calling you all night and morning," she said with a serious expression.

Maceo sighed and shuffled in his seat. He never anticipated being interrogated. "Come on with the fuckin' questions, Nadia," he said in an irritated tone. "I'm here with you right here and right now. That's all that matters," he told her. "Can I enjoy this moment with my woman without her gettin' some shit started?"

Nadia squinted her eyes. She always did that every time an attitude was brewing. "I'm not stupid, Maceo," she said in a thick Spanish accent. Her accent always seemed twice as noticeable every time she got pissed off. "I'm not stupid at all," she said before taking a sip of her wine.

***

A week later, Dre sat in a floral recliner chair as he listened to the sound of locks being unlocked. He was not as worried as he should have been. Lola had taken heed to his warning, and not once had she tried anything funny other than the one moment when she had attempted to call the police.

Dre resumed freaking the Black N' Mild as Lola entered her once peaceful and "fugitive free" home. Her gaze instantly wandered over to Dre who cracked a slight smirk. She rolled her eyes wishing he would just fall over and die from an aneurysm or sudden heart attack.

Lola knew she was wrong for thinking something so cruel, but to say she hated Dre was an understatement. Who the hell did he think he was barging into her life and home? She did not deserve any of this. She already had enough to worry about as far as work and bills. Everyday Lola thought Dre might just up and leave, he seemed to make himself more and more comfortable.

"Hey honey," Dre teased. "How was your day?"

Lola rolled her eyes and didn't respond.

Suddenly, Nina skipped over towards Dre, and hopped in his lap. She then shoved a manila paper in his face. "Look what I made in school today," she boasted.

Nina was far too young to understand the situation that was occurring around her. Instead of viewing Dre as a dangerous, wanted fugitive she instead saw him as an innocent friend of her mother's.

Dre carefully took the paper from Nina and looked over her colorful crayon creation. "You made this?" he asked. "This is really cool."

"Yeah, I made it in art class," Nina told him.

Lola looked as if she were ready to faint. She all but raced over to Dre and yanked Nina out of his lap. "Go to your room," she demanded.

"But mama—"

"Go to your room!" Lola said with finality.

The corner of Dre's lip curved into a smile. Lola looked down at him in disgust. Once Nina was out of earshot she spoke again. "Look, I've been more than cooperative," she said. "I haven't gone to the authorities."

"And I appreciate that," Dre said nonchalantly.

Lola folded her arms. "You appreciate that?" she repeated in sarcasm. "How much longer are you going to be here?" she demanded to know. "Because frankly I'd *appreciate* for you to leave."

Dre's expression was serious. "I need time to figure out what my next move is going to be."

"Well, how much longer are you going to need Mr. *DeAndre McCall*?" she asked emphasizing his name. Lola had watched the news stories on Dre and knew exactly who he was and what he was capable of. "Is it going to be weeks? Months?" she asked. "Look, no one even knows you're here. Please just leave," Tears spilled over Lola's lower lids. "Just leave. Please. I'm begging you," she cried. "I promise I won't tell a soul you were ever here."

Dre grimaced. "You done?" he asked unsympathetically.

If looks could kill, Lola would have murdered Dre a dozen times over. She quickly stormed off sulking to herself.

***

Hassan stood on the balcony of his luxury apartment and stared at the beautiful Mediterranean Sea. His open white button down shirt blew slightly in the wind. His bare chest was on full display. Seagulls gawked in the distance in a soothing manner. A few tourists relaxed on their backs while floating atop their surf boards.

Hassan had fled to Barcelona the minute he had gotten his hands back on the money. He desperately wanted to get far away from Cleveland, Ohio, and all chaos that had happened there. He figured that once he left the country the nightmares would stop and he would finally be able to sleep again.

Hassan quickly realized how wrong he had been.

He lifted the ice cold Spanish beer to his lips and took a sip. *I've got the money. I've got my freedom. I'm living stress free.*

Hassan leaned against the balcony's railing and continued to stare at the beautiful sea. Tiny waves rippled the waters.

So why the hell do I still feel unhappy, he asked himself.

***

Nikki tightened the hood around her head as she walked to the nearby convenience store. The sun was just beginning to set. It was freezing cold outside, but Nikki was unfazed by the weather. Depression was getting the best of her. The increasing loneliness she felt had her thinking and behaving irrationally.

Dre was dead. Hassan was somewhere out there. And here she was...alone and pregnant. Nikki felt sick to her stomach just thinking about her pregnancy. If she wasn't in the predicament that she was she would have gotten an abortion without hesitation. Nikki hated the fact that a life was growing inside of her. Her baby would not have a father. She didn't know the first thing about being a mother—since her own had been such a horrible one—and right now she just wanted the thing out of her. As a matter of fact, Nikki was planning on drinking enough liquor to hopefully miscarry.

Nikki hadn't saw Maceo in a week, and she still didn't have the documentation she needed to leave the country—but when the time came she didn't want to be with a child any longer. It may have seemed selfish but it was truly the way she felt.

Nikki quickly made her way towards the door, and opened it. A bell above the door chimed signaling her entrance. However before she could take a full step inside a tall, lanky brown skinned guy stepped in front of her. He looked to be in his early twenties.

"Excuse me," Nikki said in a small voice as she attempted to step around him.

The tall, lanky guy quickly moved in the same direction she had just stepped.

"Excuse me," Nikki repeated trying to step around him again.

He quickly stepped in her path once more.

Nikki looked up into the face of the annoying man who obviously wanted some form of attention. His eyes were glassy, and she could smell the liquor on his breath. It wasn't even five o'clock yet, and this motherfucker was already intoxicated.

"Please," Nikki said in a calm tone. "Get the fuck outta my way. I don't feel like playing right now."

"You too good to take two seconds to talk to me."

Nikki made a face. "I don't know you nor do I want to now move."

The cashier was too busy fetching a bottle of liquor for a customer at the counter to notice the young guy harassing Nikki.

She tried to step around him again, but he quickly stepped right back in her path.

Nikki sighed in frustration. "Did you hear me? I said move."

Suddenly, the guy snatched Nikki's arm aggressively. "Lil' dyke lookin' bitch!" he slurred.

"*Aye*! Leave her the fuck alone!" a familiar female voice said.

The young guy harassing Nikki turned around. Nikki couldn't help but to look around him to see the woman who had just stood up for her.

Much to Nikki's surprise, Quita stood several feet away. Both her hands were propped on her hips and on her beautiful dark skinned face was a no nonsense expression. Nikki was shocked that Quita would even take up for her after their last encounter. The two women had made it perfectly clear that they weren't particularly fond of each other.

Quita patted her tan shoulder purse. "Unless you wanna deal with this .38," she added.

The guy looked absolutely pissed after the threat. It was obvious that he wanted to say something, but instead he stepped out of Nikki's way and left the store without another word. Nikki looked at Quita who stared intently back at her. They did not say a word to each other as they communicated silently with their eyes. Quita slowly made her way out of the store with her bottle of Carlos Rossi Sangrea in tow.

The cashier finally made his way back to the counter—after all the drama had surpassed—and Nikki slowly made her way over making sure to keep her head down.

"What can I get you?" the cashier asked.

"I need something one-hundred proof..."

***

Clutching tightly onto the brown paper bag, Nikki quickly made her way back to the motel. Less than a quarter mile from the motel, a police cruiser suddenly pulled alongside the curb. There were no sirens or flashing lights accompanied by their presence.

Nikki stopped in her tracks automatically. Her heart felt like it had sunk into her stomach.

20

Nikki watched as two officers stepped out of the squad car. One was a black guy that appeared to be in his early forties while the other was Caucasian and looked to be in his mid-twenties.

Nikki's heart hammered rapidly in her chest. *This is it,* she thought. *This is the moment I've tried so desperately to avoid.*

The two officers slowly approached Nikki. "Evening ma'am," the black officer greeted.

Nikki opened her mouth to respond, but was unable to. She didn't know what exactly to say. She had no idea what was in store for her.

"What are you doing out here walking all alone?" the Caucasian officer asked.

Nikki licked her dry lips. She was scared out of her mind, and even contemplated running although she knew she wouldn't get too far. "I…uh…I…just…I just came from the store," she stammered. "That isn't a crime is it?" she challenged. Bad idea.

"Oh yeah? Well what you got there?" Suddenly the Caucasian officer snatched the brown bag out of Nikki's hand and peered inside. "Absolut Vodka," he read.

The black officer cut his eyes at Nikki. "Ma'am, I'm gonna have to ask you to remove your hood," he told her. "I'd like to get a good look at your face."

Nikki stood there speechless for several seconds. She didn't budge an inch. She was extremely terrified.

"Did you hear the man?!" the white officer barked. "He asked you to remove the damn hood!"

Nikki's eyes darted between the cops. Her fingers trembled at her sides but she still didn't move.

"Get your ass over here!" the white officer snapped. He yanked Nikki towards him and roughly snatched her hood off. "Yeah...just like I thought," he said.

The black officer grinned mischievously. "Put her ass in the back," he said coolly.

***

Nikki quickly sat up in her seat alert and aware that something obviously wasn't right the moment the police cruiser pulled into a dark and deserted alley.

Nikki quickly began to panic. "Where are we?" she asked fearful of the cops' intentions. "What's this? What the fuck is this shit?!"

The cruiser came to a slow stop, and at that moment Nikki really began to feel uncomfortable.

"Answer me you motherfuckers!" Nikki screamed. "Why are we here?!"

Both officers stepped out simultaneously. The white officer opened the back door, and instinctively, Nikki scooted against the opposite door. "Don't touch me!"

"Get your fucking ass over here!" he spat. He grabbed her by the legs and roughly snatched her out the back seat.

"What are you doing?!" Nikki yelled. "Why did you bring me here?!" She cried. "*Somebody help me*! Help—"

Without warning, she was suddenly hit upside the head and knocked unconscious...

***

Nikki's eyelids fluttered as she fought to regain consciousness. Her head throbbed in pain, and her vision was blurry.

Soft moans escaped from Nikki as she slowly came to. She quickly noticed several blurry figures staring at her.

"Mmmm," she groaned in pain. "Where...where am I?" she asked. Nikki tried to move her arms, but quickly noticed she was immobile. "What the fuck is going on?" she asked beginning to panic. Her vision slowly became clearer.

Lexer took slow steps towards Nikki. The heels of his Forzieri leather dress shoes click-clacked against the ground.

Nikki's heart pounded ferociously in her chest. She quickly looked up and realized her wrists were bound together using a nylon rope that was wrapped around a rusty pipe. Her feet barely touched the oil stained ground beneath her.

"What the hell is this shit?" Nikki asked panic-stricken.

Her eyes darted around her surroundings. Evidently, they were in an abandoned warehouse. Her gaze then wandered over towards the two police officers who stood nearby with her their hands clasped in front of them wearing grim expressions on their faces.

"You dirty fucking crooked ass cops!" she yelled.

Both cops chuckled amused by her temperament.

Lexer had all kinds of people working for him so it was not a problem to get police officers to pull a few strings for him. Besides, money spoke volumes. He and Nikki had unfinished business to tend to and once he deemed she was no longer useful, authorities could do with her whatever they pleased. But until then, her ass was his.

"I've been looking for you, Nikita Brown," Lexer said in that deep, ghoulish voice that made the hairs on the back of Nikki's neck stand. "You aren't an easy woman to track down," he told her."

"Who the fuck are you?" Nikki's voice was a combination of fear and anger.

Lexer stood less than a foot away from her. "I can be your worse fucking nightmare if you make this any harder than it has to be."

"I'm not fucking scared of you," Nikki spat.

WHAP!

Lexer slapped the shit out of Nikki before she even saw it coming!

"You should be bitch!" He was a man who rarely if ever raised his voice, but he was finally becoming tired of the games and bullshit. He wanted the money that was owed to him, and he wanted it now.

Nikki's cheek stung from the vicious blow.

"Where's. My. Money." Lexer paused between each word he said to add emphasis.

"What money—"

WHAP!

Lexer's palm connected with Nikki's cheek once more. Blood began to leak from her nostrils after the blow.

"I'm going to ask you one more time," he said through gritted teeth. "Where's my money?"

Nikki slowly eyed each man in the room. There were a total of six. Her gaze then connected with Lexer's yellow tinted eyes. "Go fuck yourself," she muttered.

Lexer couldn't believe how hardheaded Nikki was behaving, but he knew a sure way to let her know that he wasn't playing.

After snatching his gun out, he shoved the barrel beneath Nikki's chin.

She instantly tensed up. Fear swept her features as her life flashed before her eyes. "I don't have the money," she quickly said. "But I know who does."

Lexer stared into Nikki's hazel eyes for several seconds as he tried to read her. Satisfied with her response he spoke again. "I'm going to give you a fair chance to make things right," he spoke to her. "And that's something I rarely do."

Blood seeped down Nikki's lips and ran down her chin. Blood dripped off her chin and landed on the toe of Lexer's Italian designer shoes.

"I'm giving you forty-eight hours to come up with my fucking money," he explained. "Or else I'm coming for your ass."

One of Lexer's bodyguards made his way over towards Nikki; using a switchblade he cut her loose. She dropped to the dirty ground and wiped the blood from beneath her nose.

Lexer bent down and roughly snatched Nikki's head back by her hair. She instantly yelped in pain. "You don't wanna fuck with me," he told her.

21

"How long is your friend going to stay here?" Nina asked.

Lola pulled the Spongebob sheet over her daughter and carefully tucked her in. "That's not...um...that's not mommy's friend baby," she explained to her daughter.

Nina's eyebrows furrowed in confusion. "Then who is he mommy?" she asked.

Lola sighed in frustration. Nina was just too young to comprehend what was going on and Lola had no intentions of explaining it. "He's um," she paused. "Just a visitor," she finally answered. "He's just visiting."

Nina smiled. "Well, I like him."

Lola sat speechless for several seconds. If only Nina knew...because if she did she would hate Dre just as much as her mother did.

"Get some sleep, okay?" she said before placing a soft kiss on her daughter's forehead.

"Good night," Nina said.

"Night, baby," Lola told her daughter.

She then stood to her feet and headed towards the door—her lips curved into a frown after she noticed

Dre had been standing there for only God knew how long.

Dre cracked a smirk and Lola immediately caught an attitude. She quickly made her way past him as if he weren't there.

Knock!

Knock!

Knock!

"*Who's that*?" Dre quickly asked.

"I don't know," Lola mumbled.

Dre walked behind Lola, grabbed her by the forearm, and whirled her around to face him. "You called the police?" he demanded to know.

Lola snatched her hand out of his grasp. "No, I didn't," she said through gritted teeth. "I don't know who it is."

Dre's first thought was to grab his piece, but then he realized he was weaponless. *Damn, I have to hit up Maceo,* he told himself. Dre knew it wasn't in his best interest to not have a gun for protection. He would rather be safe than sorry.

Dre slowly followed behind Lola, but kept a safe distance. If she had in fact contacted the police he would make a quick run for the back door. The police had life all the way messed up if they thought they would easily apprehend Dre.

Lola peered through the peephole and sighed dejectedly.

"Who is it?" Dre whispered in the distance. His nerves were understandably on edge.

"It's my baby daddy," Lola answered unenthusiastically.

Dre looked irritated. "Yo, what the fuck is he doin' comin' over at this time of night?" he asked.

Lola didn't respond as she unlocked her door but cracked it slightly. "What do you want, Ricardo?" she asked.

Ricardo was Nina's father as well as a married man. Unfortunately, Lola knew nothing of his marriage and other children until after she had pushed out Nina in a hospital delivery room. She had never been the same due to Ricardo's betrayal, and he was mostly guilty for her cold, emotionless demeanor towards men.

Lola had given her heart to a man who had promised to wed her as soon as their child was born, but instead had left her on her own to raise their daughter. She was a fool in love who had fallen prey to a smooth talking, pretty boy that had sold her romantic dreams. Lola had been floating on cloud nine only to land flat on her ass.

"I just wanna talk to you baby," Ricardo explained.

The moment Lola got a whiff of Ricardo's breath she could tell that he had been drinking. "It's too late to talk," she told him.

They stared at each other in silence for several seconds. Ricardo was a very handsome man. His looks were what attracted Lola in the first place. Ricardo had rich, smooth caramel skin, and wore his hair cut low. A neatly trimmed mustache and goatee surrounded his full lips. He had a beautiful pair of dark brown eyes that could persuade any woman to do just about anything without even uttering a word. Ricardo was a pretty boy and he knew it. He was also an alcoholic and abuser. Lola tried her hardest to forget those painful memories.

"Fine," Ricardo said. "Well at least let me see Nina."

"Nina's asleep," Lola said clearly agitated.

"You know she's my daughter too," Ricardo slurred. He was pissy drunk. The scent of alcohol reeked from his pores.

"Ricardo, you're drunk. Go home to your wife," Lola said before closing the door.

Ricardo suddenly stopped her by placing his hand on the door. "I want to come in," he told her. "I want to hold you until you fall asleep. You remember, Lol'? Like how I used to do?"

"No, Ricardo," Lola said. "Just go home, okay?" she told him. This wasn't Ricardo's first time showing up at her doorstep in the middle of the night drunk, and she wasn't proud to admit that a few times she had even allowed him entrance. But now things were different...she was different.

Ricardo however was not going to leave easily. "Do you have a man in there?" he demanded to know. "That must be what it is. You gotta man in there?!"

"Keep your voice down before you wake the neighbors," Lola said.

"Well then let me in," Ricardo said.

"I'm closing the door now," Lola told him. "Move your hand—"

"Open the fucking door!" Ricardo demanded.

"You're not coming in—"

Ricardo reached through the small opening in the door and grabbed a fistful of Lola's hair. "You're too good for me now bitch?!" he yelled.

Lola cried out in pain as Ricardo yanked on her locks.

Dre quickly intervened. After prying Ricardo's fingers off Lola's hair, he opened the door wide enough to shove the hell out of Ricardo. He stumbled backwards almost falling to the ground.

"The fuck outta here, nigga!" Dre yelled.

Ricardo backed away obviously not wanting any trouble with the six feet two inch, two-hundred and twenty pound man.

"And don't bring ya punk ass back here!" Dre told him.

Ricardo shook his head and chuckled in disbelief. "And you got *me* paying child support?" he asked in a sarcastic tone.

"It's the least you should be able to do," Lola spoke up as she wiped tears from her eyes. "It's not like you take care of your daughter."

"Why should I when you got him?!" Ricardo pointed to Dre.

Lola shook her head in amazement. "You're so fucking petty, Ricardo. Grow up. Don't ever come here again."

"Ya ass got two seconds to roll out," Dre threatened.

Ricardo only needed one as he hopped inside his 2010 Ford Taurus and skirted off. Dre and Lola watched as his car disappeared in the distance. She could not believe Ricardo had the nerve to show up to her house and disrespect her.

Dre turned towards Lola. "You aight?" he asked in a concerned tone.

Lola tucked her hair behind her ear and looked down at the ground. "Yes," she said in a low tone. "Thank you..."

Dre placed his hand on her back. "Come on. Let's go back inside."

***

Maceo walked across the motel parking lot to Nikki's motel room carrying a large manila envelope. He hadn't spoken to her in a week, and honestly he needed to put a little space between them. Maceo wasn't used to a woman staying on his mind as much as Nikki did, and truthfully he wasn't digging the effect she had on him. He needed to gain control of the situation quickly before he did something that he regretted, and separating himself for a little while helped him do just that.

Once Maceo reached Nikki's door, he inserted his keycard. He could not wait to show her what was inside the envelope. Maceo pushed the door open.

Nikki's meager attire only consisted of a pair of jeans a black bra. She had just cracked open the bottle of Absolut—which the cops were so "gracious" enough to return—and was now pouring herself a shot.

Maceo closed the door behind himself, tossed the manila envelope on the nearby table, and slowly approached Nikki. "What are you doing?" he asked. He was clearly bothered by what he was seeing.

Nikki ignored his question as she lifted the Styrofoam cup.

Suddenly, Maceo slapped the drink out of her hand! The cup flew halfway across the motel room, the contents spilling onto the carpet.

"What the fuck do you care for?!" Nikki yelled. "You act like it's your fucking baby!"

Maceo surprised himself and Nikki when he suddenly grabbed her by the face and crushed his lips against hers. He half expected Nikki to stop him or push him away, but she did neither. Maceo towered over Nikki by more than a foot. Her body seemingly melted into his as their kiss turned from aggression into passion.

Maceo's dick pressed against the denim fabric of his jeans as he sucked on Nikki's bottom lip. Soft whimpers escaped her lips as she indulged in a powerful kiss that had been a long time in the making.

Suddenly, he lifted Nikki up placing soft kisses against her lips one after the other. Her legs wrapped around his body, his strong, buff arms held her by her tiny waist. Maceo slowly walked over towards the bed.

He carefully laid her delicate body on the bed, and climbed on top of her. Nikki's back arched as Maceo proceeded to slowly kiss her body in a downward motion. Once he reached her waist, he unfastened and unzipped her jeans. Nikki's heart rate sped up. Her mind was telling her to stop him, but her body yearned for what Maceo was about to give her.

Nikki lifted her backside as Maceo tugged her jeans down her legs. She bit her bottom lip as he began to place soft, slow kisses on her inner thigh, swirling his tongue in circular motions along her velvet skin.

Nikki ran her hands over Maceo's smooth bald head. His beard tickled her skin in delicate spots, and it all felt very intoxicating.

"*Mmm,*" she whimpered.

Maceo slowly eased Nikki's black panties down her legs and tossed them onto the carpet. He spread her legs as far apart as her flexibility would allow before burying his face in her pussy.

Nikki arched her back and grabbed Maceo's bald head. "*Oooohhh,*" she moaned.

He sucked expertly on her swollen clit, dipping his tongue inside her slick opening every now and then.

Nikki's cheeks flushed as he devoured her pussy much like they had been longtime lovers.

Maceo slipped his hands underneath Nikki's buttock and lifted her upward slightly, pressing her pelvis firmly against his face. He ate her kitty as if it was his last meal on Earth. His soft groans turned Nikki on even more as he licked, lapped, and sucked aggressively.

Nikki's fingernails dug slightly into Maceo's scalp. She tried to inch away a little. The pleasure was damn near unbearable. Maceo tightened his hold on her securing her in place. He pulled her back where she belonged and continued to feast on her drenched pussy. He absolutely loved the way she tasted.

Nikki bucked and jerked as she felt a powerful climax approaching. She encased her bottom lip and grabbed a handful of the white sheets. "I'm about to cum," she moaned.

Maceo licked and sucked faster and harder on her pearl. Her toes curled as her face twisted up. "*Oooohhh*!" she cried out. A powerful orgasm suddenly shook her senses.

Maceo slowly lifted his head and wiped his wet lips. His full beard was filled with traces of Nikki's juices, but he didn't care. He climbed back into the bed and lay beside a panting Nikki.

She reached down and slowly began to unfasten his jeans. Their lips met for a series of passionate kisses. Nikki sucked greedily on Maceo's tongue tasting her own sweet nectar. She could not move fast enough as she unzipped his jeans.

Maceo suddenly pulled back, and stopped her from going any further. "Hol' up. Hol' up, ma," he said.

"What's wrong?" Nikki asked breathlessly.

He shook his head, looked down, and scratched the bridge of his nose. "Real talk, Nikki, you don't wanna get involved with a nigga like me," he warned her.

Nikki reached inside his jeans and caressed his thick dick through his cotton boxers. "Maybe I do," she whispered. "I need this..." She knew she was behaving messy, but they had already come this far. Why stop now? She wanted Maceo, and it was obvious that he wanted her. "I wanna feel you," Nikki whispered.

Maceo leaned down and kissed her soft lips passionately.

"You've been so good to me," she told him a low tone. Suddenly, she mounted him. Maceo watched as she slowly undid her bra, and tossed it casually on the floor. She lifted his hands and placed his palms against her small breasts.

Maceo softly massaged them in his large hands. He closed his eyes as she grinded her bare pussy against his erection which was threatening to burst through the seams of his jeans

She slowly brought his right hand to her lips and seductively trailed her tongue along each of his fingertips. Maceo no longer had any restraint left in him.

He carefully lifted her off him and placed her onto her back before climbing on top of her. After freeing himself of his jeans and boxers, he slipped inside her wetness. Nikki's legs tightened around Maceo's waist as her fingernails dug into his back.

"*Aaaahh*!" she cried out.

Maceo filled her with deep, circular strokes as he placed soft kisses along her neck and jawline.

"*Fuck*!" Nikki moaned.

***

"*Fuck*!" Nadia yelled.

She sat at the dining room table all alone in the dark. The only light that illuminated the room were the candles lit on her birthday cake. Tears slipped from her eyes as she stared at the beautiful personal cake decorated in pink hearts. Mascara ran down her cheeks but she didn't bother wiping it away.

Standing to her feet, Nadia leaned over the small cake and blew the candles out. *Fuck love,* she said to herself. Suddenly, Nadia grabbed the nearby ten inch butcher knife and viciously stabbed the birthday cake several times!

"*Fuck you*! *Fuck you*! *Fuck you*! *Fuck you motherfucker*!" she screamed. Nadia then tossed the knife, picked up the birthday cake and hauled it halfway across the room.

Her temper tantrum didn't just stop there. Nadia kicked over several dining chairs in a fit of rage. She then walked over to the nearest wall and pressed her back against it as she cried hysterically. She slid downward on the wall wallowing in her own lonely sorrows. Nadia could not believe that Maceo had forgotten all about her birthday.

22

The sound of Maceo's cell phone vibrating on the nightstand awoke him two hours later. He wiped his eyes, and looked over his shoulder at Nikki who was fast asleep. Maceo reached over and retrieved his cellphone. He was expecting to see Nadia's number flashing across his screen, but instead it was an unrecognizable number. The area code was 216 so the call was local.

Assuming that it might be money, Maceo decided to answer it. "Hello?" he answered in a muffled voice.

"A nigga need you to come through for him," a recognizable voice said. "Some fucked up shit went down..."

Maceo sat up in bed, and swung his legs around. "Who is this?" he asked.

There was a slight pause on the other end. "...Dre..."

Maceo pulled the phone away from his face and stared at it for several seconds. He had to have been hearing shit. "Dre who?" he asked. The Dre *he* knew was dead last he checked.

"DeAndre...come on nigga. Dre...you know me..."

Maceo shook his head. It sounded like Dre, but it was impossible for it to be him. Nikki had told him that she witnessed Hassan empty a clip into his boy. "Nah," Maceo said. "This can't be my nigga Dre," he said.

"Dawg, Hassan flipped and turned on us," Dre said. "The nigga shot me, and um…I'm not sure, but I think he killed Nikki…" His voice cracked with that statement.

Maceo sighed dejectedly, and ran a hand over his face and beard. He couldn't believe what he was hearing. Maceo then turned and looked over his shoulder at Nikki. She was still fast asleep.

"I thought you were dead," Maceo told Dre.

"Nah…a nigga just been out of the loop," Dre explained. "But I'm back, and I wanna find this mothafucka and put a bullet in his head," he told Maceo. "But first thing's first…I need a gun…and hopefully a lil' paper if you can throw that my way. You know I got you when I get back on my feet, bro'."

Maceo looked over his shoulder at Nikki once more. He knew the right thing to do was to tell Dre that Nikki was not dead. In fact she was lying right next to him…but Maceo refused to do just that.

"Aight," Maceo agreed. "I'ma hit you hit back at this number in a few hours."

"Bet," Dre agreed.

Maceo then disconnected the call.

***

The sunlight pouring into the motel room shined bright on Nikki's face. Slowly stirring awake, she cracked her eyes open. Her pupils fought to adjust to the sunlight. Holding a hand up to block the fierce brightness, Nikki sat up in bed.

"Mornin'," Maceo greeted. He walked over to the mini-fridge and pulled out two Snapple apple juices. "How'd you sleep?" he asked.

Nikki's eyes scanned his chiseled bare chest. He wore only a pair of Levis jeans. "I…um…I slept pretty well." She cleared her throat. She was half expecting him to comment on the steamy events from last night.

Maceo handed her a Snapple.

Nikki twisted off the cap, and took a small sip of the cold beverage. After replacing the cap, she sat the bottle on the nightstand. She wore an uncomfortable expression, and it was obvious that something was on her mind.

Maceo immediately took note of her sudden mood change. "You good?" he asked. He took a seat in the chair. Maceo assumed Nikki was regretting everything that had taken place between them last night. He figured her conscience would eventually set in.

Nikki slightly hesitated. She wasn't quite sure how to say it. "Yesterday, when I was walking back to the motel," she began. "A police car rolled up on me."

Maceo's eyebrows furrowed as he listened intently to Nikki's story.

“They hopped out the car, asked me a couple questions, next thing I know I’m in the back of the cruiser getting hauled off,” she told him. “Right then and there, I just knew my life was coming to an end. I was telling myself ‘this is it. I’m going to prison.’”

“So how’d you get ya ass outta there?” Maceo asked.

“They didn’t take me to the police station,” she explained. “They knocked me out cold, and the next thing I knew I woke up in a fucking warehouse tied up. Some tall, creepy, motherfucker—I don’t even know his name,” she said. “Anyway he told me that I had two days to get his money to him or else he’d come looking for me.”

Maceo raised an eyebrow. “Money?” he asked confused. “What money?”

“At first I wasn’t even sure about what the hell money he was talking about,” she said. “But I think he’s referring to the money Dre, Hassan, and I stole from Timothy’s safe. It’s the only thing I can think of.”

“Nikki, why didn’t you tell me this shit yesterday?” Maceo asked clearly agitated.

Nikki drew her knees up to her chest. She looked away unable to meet Maceo’s intense gaze. “I’ve been hiding something else from you,” she admitted in a low tone.

Maceo grimaced. “And what’s that?”

Nikki slowly climbed out the bed, and retrieved the bag of money underneath the mattress. She then dumped the contents onto the bed.

Maceo watched as stacks of money fell onto the mattress. He knew how Nikki got down so the first thought that came to his mind was that she had robbed a bank. “Where’d you get all that money?” he asked in disbelief.

Nikki drew in a deep breath and then went on to explain the brief encounter with Hassan. By the time she finished telling the story Maceo was in total shock and amazement.

“Hassan has the rest,” Nikki said.

Maceo sat speechless for several seconds shaking his head.

“I’m sorry I didn’t tell you all this sooner,” she apologized. “Are you upset with me?”

“I’m just mad you ain’t put a bullet in that nigga after everything he did to you,” Maceo said.

Nikki flopped down onto the mattress and shook her head. “You don’t understand,” she told him. “It’s not as simple as you think…”

“What the hell is so hard about putting your finger on a trigger and squeezing it?” Maceo asked in a sarcastic tone.

"The gun was in my hand," she told him. "My finger was on the trigger. But..." Her voice trailed off.

"But?" Maceo asked.

"My heart wasn't in it," Nikki confessed.

Maceo snorted and shook his head. "You sound like you got a soft spot for this nigga," he said.

Nikki quickly looked away, and that small gesture explained everything. Maceo shook his head in disbelief. He instantly began to put two and two together, but he decided against speaking on it. Whatever had transpired between Nikki, Dre, and Hassan had nothing to do with him. Besides it was neither here nor there.

"I'm afraid of that man...," Nikki whispered referring to Lexer. It was something about him that put fear in her heart.

"Look, I can call my boys and we can handle this shit," Maceo said.

"No," Nikki quickly said. "You don't know this guy, Maceo. He's got the fucking police working for him and shit. He's not somebody you wanna fuck with. Trust me," she added.

"Well, that mothafucka ain't gon' get a chance to lay a hand on you," Maceo told her. He stood to his feet, grabbed the manila envelope off the table, and made his way towards her. "I got somethin' for you."

"What's this?" Nikki asked taking the envelope.

"Open it," he simply said.

She quickly tore open the envelope and pulled out her new identification. A birth certificate, social security card, and even a license. "Kelly Carter," she read the name. A smile tugged at her lips. "I always hated the name Kelly," she teased.

"Really?" Maceo asked smiling. "I thought it fit you."

Nikki beamed as she stared at the documents. Now she could finally get far away from all the drama, chaos, and most importantly the police. She would finally be able to live again without having to look over her shoulder during every move she made.

"Don't worry about that nigga, aight?" Maceo said in a reassuring tone. "And that nigga, Hassan, he don't want no smoke for real. Don't even sweat none of that shit. You're straight now."

Nikki hopped off the bed, ran up to Maceo, and pulled in him for a passionate kiss. "Thank you," she told him. "For everything."

Maceo stared deep into Nikki's beautiful eyes. "I told you," he said. "I got ya back."

Nikki slowly pulled him in for another kiss. Maceo's cell phone began vibrating on the nightstand but he didn't even hear it. Nikki had his undivided attention.

His caller ID indicated that Nadia was calling. She was beginning to get hysterical because of his absence. First he had missed her birthday, and now he hadn't even bothered coming back home. She didn't know what Maceo was on, but she wasn't feeling it.

Maceo slowly backed Nikki up towards the bed. She flopped back onto the bed while he stood in front of her. She slowly began unfastening his jeans.

"You sure you wanna do this again?" Maceo asked.

Nikki ignored his question as she unzipped his jeans and tugged them down his toned legs. He stepped out of the jeans and slowly joined her in bed. The mattress creaked beneath his weight as he climbed on top of her. Nikki quickly wiggled out of her panties and spread her thighs welcoming Maceo to cross her threshold.

Nikki gasped upon his deep penetration. She felt so good to Maceo. So warm, tight, and wet. He could stay planted right there in the same position until the sun set.

"Damn...," Maceo groaned. "Whatchu' doin' to me, girl?" he asked.

Nikki grinded her hips against his. "I don't know what I'm doing to you," she told him. "But I know what you're doing to me."

Maceeo slid farther inside Nikki as he slid his tongue in her mouth. They kissed passionately until they had no choice but to pull apart to catch their breath.

"I told you last night," he said. "You don't wanna fall for a nigga like me..."

She planted a soft kiss against Maceo's lips. "I know you won't let me hit the ground..."

***

Nadia wore a pair of black Helianthe sneakers, a pair of skin tight jeans, and a black leather jacket as she stormed into The Spot II bar on Kinsman Avenue. It was a place that Maceo usually hung out at. She considered her clothing as her "fighting attire" because she had a feeling she was going to end up whupping some hoe's ass.

Nadia didn't spot Maceo in the bar, but she expected as much since she didn't see his car parked along the street. She did, however, see his homie AJ sitting at the bar watching the football game on television while sipping on a Budweiser.

She quickly made her way over towards him. A few fellas turned their heads in her direction. Wherever Nadia went, she drew attention without evening having to try.

Most of the guys missed the touchdown that had just been scored because they were too busy eyeing Nadia's large, round ass in the skin tight jeans.

"Yo, AJ?" she called out as she approached him.

He turned in Nadia's direction. "What's good?" he asked. He didn't expect Nadia to be here.

"You talked to Maceo lately?" she asked. "I can't find him anywhere."

AJ hesitated. Nadia and Maceo's personal affairs were none of his business. "I don't know nothin' 'bout that," he said.

Nadia wasn't convinced. "Where is he, AJ?" she asked. "I know you know. He's your homie. You both kick it like every day so I know you would know if he was laid up with some bitch right now," she said. "Is he with Quita?"

AJ took a swig from his beer. "I told you I don't know."

Nadia sighed in frustration. Obviously it was time for plan B. She pulled out a small wad of cash from her jacket's pocket and handed it to AJ.

"What's this?" he asked dumbfounded.

"He doesn't have to know you told me, AJ." Nadia looked down at the money and then back at AJ. "You take care of me, and I'll take care of you."

AJ grimaced. He would much rather *take care* of something else, but Maceo would kill him if he even looked at Nadia the wrong way.

AJ took the small wad of money from Nadia. “He’s at the Kirkland Inn Motel with some chick named Nikki.”

Nadia smiled sadistically. *People would do anything for the right price,* she thought to herself.

She then turned and left the bar. Maceo had another thing coming if he thought Nadia wasn’t going to go looking for him. He should have known his girl better than that.

***

“I got a few moves to make,” Maceo explained as he dressed. He still had no intentions of telling Nikki that Dre had contacted him last night, and that he was in fact still alive. “Couple people to catch up with, then tomorrow morning we’ll get on the road.”

Nikki pulled her shirt on. “We?” she asked confused.

“Well, how else you thought you was gon’ get ya ass out the country?” he asked.

BOOM!

BOOM!

BOOM!

Nikki and Maceo’s attention quickly focused on the door. Someone was knocking loud as hell. As a matter of fact it didn’t even sound like a knock, it sounded as if someone was literally kicking the door.

Nikki's heart instantly dropped into the pit of her stomach. Her first thought was that it was the police. She figured someone had probably pointed the authorities right where she was located. She then thought about Lexer...

23

Maceo held up his hand signaling silence from Nikki.

BOOM!

BOOM!

BOOM!

The door continued to get assaulted as Nikki and Maceo tried to figure out who was on the opposite side.

Maceo slowly made his way towards the door, and opened it against his better judgment. He cracked the door open two inches, but Nadia suddenly burst inside!

"Where is she you piece of shit?!" She screamed.

"Nadia, what the fuck are you doin'?!" Maceo yelled.

She looked up into her man's face. "What am I doing?! I sat up and waited for you triflin' ass all n—" Nadia's voice trailed off the moment she noticed Nikki standing less than several feet away. "So this is the hoe?" she asked with a disgusted look on her face. "You want this average bitch over all this?!" she screamed.

"Nadia, chill the fuck out for somebody call the police!"

"Don't you tell me to fucking chill out! I could kill you!" she screamed. Tears and mascara ran down her ivory skin as she cried hysterically.

Suddenly, Nadia brandished the Glock 26 Maceo had gotten her for her birthday last year.

Nikki quickly backed up. *What the hell is this chick on,* she thought to herself.

"Whoa! Whoa! Nadia, what the fuck?!" Maceo yelled.

Nadia quickly pointed her gun in his face. "I stayed up all night waiting for your sorry ass!" she screamed. "It was my fucking birthday you asshole! And what were you doing?!" she shouted. "You were too busy screwing this average ass black bitch! Well I hope it was good for you motherfucker!"

"Nadia, man, I'm tellin' ya ass right now. Get that fuckin' gun out my face!" Maceo warned her.

The gun trembled in her hands as she aimed it with purpose. Mascara and tears stained her cheeks. Her nostrils flared wildly. Nadia didn't even look like herself. Instead she looked much like a deranged woman. Love could be such a bitch.

Without warning, Nadia suddenly aimed the gun in Nikki's direction.

Nikki's eyes widened in fear. "*Maceo*?!"

Maceo quickly leapt for the gun and grabbed it, but Nadia fought to keep possession of the gun.

"Gimme this fuckin' shit!" Maceo finally snatched the gun from her before she could fire it.

"Fuck you!" Nadia spat on Maceo. "You aren't shit! It's over!" She turned and headed for the door. "And for the record, I aborted your baby two months ago, motherfucker!"

Maceo's eyes bulged in their sockets. "Bitch, what the fuck did you just say?!" he yelled. "You did what?!"

Nadia turned on her heel and faced Maceo. "You heard me you piece of shit! I had our fucking baby aborted!"

"You lil' fuckin' hoe—bitch, I'ma whup yo' ass—"

"Maceo!" Nikki intervened. "Don't..."

Maceo instantly stopped in his tracks. If it hadn't been for Nikki speaking up, he would have been ringing Nadia's neck.

Nadia looked over at Nikki and shook her head. "You'll never be enough for a man like him," she said before walking out of the motel room.

Nikki and Maceo stood in silence for several seconds. He exhaled deeply and ran a hand over his bald head.

"This is all my fault," Nikki whispered. "We should have never—I should have never—"

"Nikki, please," Maceo cut her off. "This shit was a long time comin'. Ain't no reason to start blamin' yaself."

She slowly walked over to the bed and took a seat. "I just feel like shit," she told him. "You've been here for me since day one...I should have respected your relationship. I should have respected myself..."

Maceo sighed. "What's done is done, Nikki," he said bluntly. "We're human. We ain't meant to be perfect." He walked over towards Nikki and joined her on the bed. "We already in this shit together now, Nikki," he told her. "Ain't no need to start beatin' yaself up and regrettin' shit now."

Nikki lifted her gaze and stared into Maceo's dark brown eyes. "Look at me," she said. "I'm pregnant...and I'm a wanted fugitive on the run..."

Maceo grinned. "You're fucked up," he told her. "Like me..."

Nikki couldn't resist the smile that crept across her lips.

***

"I can't believe you're fuckin' standin' right here, nigga," Maceo said before dapping Dre up.

The two men stood in Lola's front lawn. She had stepped out to buy groceries, but Dre wasn't worried her about trying any slick shit. She was slowly but surely gaining his trust.

"Me in the flesh," Dre said. "So...um...where'd you hear I got killed?" he asked.

Maceo hesitated. "I...uh...shit, I mean I ain't never hear back from ya ass after we last saw each other. You never hit me back about the documents so I ain't know what the hell to expect. Hell, I figured the worst my nigga."

Dre nodded his head. "Yeah...I feel you. Shit, a nigga thought he was dead himself, real talk."

"So what all really happened the day of the robbery?" Maceo asked. He had already heard Nikki's version of the story now he wanted to hear Dre's.

"All the fuck I remember is running up in the nigga's shit totin' my gun, callin' shots, and then some mothafucka runs up in the house out of nowhere. Before I knew it, Hassan turned and blasted on a nigga." Dre slowly lifted his shirt revealing the many bullet wound scars that would forever remain on his skin.

"Damn," Maceo said. "You's a mothafuckin' trooper, dawg."

"You know a nigga hard to kill like Steven Seagal," Dre joked.

Maceo chuckled. "Straight up. Straight up," he agreed. "But look though, I got a lil' somethin' for you," he said before digging in his pocket. He then handed Nadia's Glock 26 to Dre.

Dre chuckled. "Nigga, what the fuck is this shit?" he asked clearly amused by the small handgun.

"I had to take this off my crazy ass girl's hands," Maceo said. "She ain't got no use for it and neither do I. I mean, it probably ain't what you used to but check it, it's free," Maceo told him. "And it serves the same purpose as every other mothafuckin' gun."

Dre nodded in agreement. "True. True."

Maceo pulled out a few hundred dollar bills and handed it to his homeboy.

"Thanks man," Dre said. "I really appreciate this shit. I really appreciate you comin' through for me."

"You know it ain't no problem—"

"I mean, I know, but I'm sayin' though we fucks with each other on a business level...but you showin' me brotherly love, and I really appreciate that shit."

Maceo and Dre dapped each other up again.

Suddenly, Lola's car pulled into the driveway of her home. The two men turned their attention towards her Honda. They watched intently as she parked, killed the engine, and climbed out. Nina anxiously hopped out the backseat.

Lola grabbed several plastic grocery bags from the backseat and quickly made her way towards the front door of her home. She didn't once make eye contact with neither Dre or Maceo.

Nina waved at Dre as she followed her mother into the house.

Maceo quietly watched the entire scene. He gave Dre a knowing look once Lola and Nina disappeared inside the house. "So *that's* what's been keepin' ya ass preoccupied," he stated.

Dre understood exactly what Maceo was driving at. "Nah, it's nothing like that," he assured him.

Maceo raised an eyebrow in skepticism. He wasn't buying that shit, but it wasn't any of his business. Right now his only concern was Nikki.

"Well, look man, I'm 'bout to roll out," Maceo said. "You hit me up if you need anything," he told Dre.

"Good lookin', bruh," Dre thanked Maceo once more.

After dapping one more time, he climbed into his car, and pulled off. There was no way in hell Maceo was going to tell Dre about Nikki. He would simply allow them to continue to believe one another was dead. Maceo truly believed he could do more for Nikki than Dre ever could. Hell, it was because of Dre that Nikki was even involved in the mess she was in. Maceo was the one picking up and putting the pieces of her once chaotic life back together.

Nikki didn't need Dre. And from the looks of Lola, Maceo believed, it was obvious Dre didn't need Nikki.

***

Dre slowly entered the kitchen. He ran a hand through his dreadlocks. They desperately needed to be re-twisted. Leaning against the door frame, he watched as Lola placed the groceries in their designated spots. Lola was quiet and seemed withdrawn. Dre wondered if the events from last night were still on her mind.

He slowly made his way inside the kitchen, and leaned against the counter. "How'd you ever get involved with a mothafucka like that?" he suddenly asked her.

The question caught Lola off guard, but she couldn't say that she wasn't expecting it sooner or later. She briefly ran down how her and Ricardo had met, but made sure to leave out vital details such as him already having a wife when they had met.

"Was he always like that?" Dre asked.

Lola stood on her tiptoes and tried to place a box in the highest shelf of a cabinet. "Was he always a jerk?" she asked. "Yes..."

"Let me get that," he said approaching her.

"I got it," Lola insisted. She pushed the box inside the cabinet, closed the door, and turned around.

Lola quickly gasped. She wasn't expecting Dre to be as close in proximity as he was. Their bodies were less than an inch apart. She could feel Dre's warm breath blowing on her as he stared down at her.

Their gazes locked, and neither of them said a word.

Dre slowly stepped closer—

"Mama." Nina stepped inside the tension-filled kitchen. "I want to go outside and play."

Lola nervously ran a hand through her long, curly hair. She then stepped around Dre and walked over towards her daughter.

Dre stared at her petite firm ass in her black jeans. *She felt it*, he told himself.

24

Maceo knocked on Quita's door, and patiently waited for her to answer it. Several seconds later, she unlatched the door and slightly cracked it open.

"What's up? Let me in," he told her.

Quita looked apprehensive. "Now's really not a good time," she said.

Maceo was taken back. "Fuck you talkin' bout?" he asked confused. "Woman, if you don't open this mothafuckin' door," he threatened.

Quita sighed, and hesitantly opened the door for Maceo to enter. After all, he did pay the bills there.

The moment Maceo stepped inside the apartment, his four year old daughter, MaKayla came running up to him with her little arms outstretched.

"Daddy! *Daddy*!" she said enthusiastically.

Maceo kneeled down and embraced his only child. She was the center of his entire world. His heart. "Hey daddy's baby!"

"Aye, Quita, where you put my razors?"

Maceo turned in the direction of Quita's company. It was the same guy whose ass he almost whupped the last time he was here.

Maceo slowly stood to his feet. Quita's friend looked from Maceo to Quita. He wore only a pair of Hanes boxer, and in his left hand was a can of Gillette shaving cream.

"Nigga, you a lil' too comfortable in this mothafucka ain't you?" Maceo asked him.

Quita's friend looked nervous. "I...uh...um—"

Without warning, Maceo rushed him, wrapped a massive hand around the shorter man's throat and slammed him against the nearest wall. The shaving cream dropped from his hand as the back of his skull smacked the wall.

Maceo then pressed his forearm against the guy's throat, crushing his windpipe.

"*Maceo*, stop!" Quita pleaded.

"Mothafucka, I oughta kill yo' ass!" Maceo yelled.

"Maceo, please! Stop!"

Maceo snatched the guy up by the nape of his neck, and literally walked him to the door. After opening it, he roughly shoved the guy into the apartment hallway. He didn't even bother letting the guy put on his clothes, but he should have felt fortunate that he still had his life.

The guy stumbled, fell onto the floor, and quickly got up and ran off.

"Don't bring yo' mothafuckin' ass back here, nigga!" Maceo shouted out after him before slamming the door.

Quita stood several feet away, twiddling her fingers, and looking absolutely terrified.

Maceo took one look at his baby mother and flipped. *"Bitch, you must've lost yo' mothafuckin' mind*!" he yelled pointing his finger at her. "I can't believe you would disrespect me and your own mothafuckin' daughter! Got this nigga walkin' around half-naked around my child! I should beat yo' mothafuckin' ass all up and down this apartment!" he threatened.

Maceo's gaze wandered over towards his daughter who looked frightened. His temper immediately dissipated. He hated for his daughter to see and hear him behaving in such a manner. MaKayla wasn't used to seeing that side of him...but Quita was.

"Come here, Kay," he ushered for her to come over.

She did, and he kneeled down, and lifted her in his arms.

Maceo walked over towards the kitchen counter and poured him a glass of Rossi from the half full bottle.

Quita exhaled deeply, and slowly walked over towards the living room sofa before taking a seat. She had been this close to getting her ass whupped.

Maceo joined her in the living room, and took a seat on the opposite couch. MaKayla rested her head on her father's chest, and relaxed.

Maceo took a long sip of the sweet wine. "I'm driving Nikki to Oaxaca," he told Quita.

"The hell is this that?" she asked.

"It's a city in southwestern Mexico," he explained. "I'll be gone for a few days."

"Mexico?" Quita repeated sarcastically.

"Well, it's not like she can stay here."

Quita scratched her scalp and sighed. "How long is it going to take you to get there?" she asked.

"A lil less than two days," he answered.

Quita stared at Maceo in disbelief. "You're jeopardizing your own freedom for this chick," she said. "This girl must really mean a lot to you..."

***

Dre knocked on Lola's open bedroom door later on that night, and slowly stepped inside. She stood in front of her dresser, brushing through her long luxurious hair while wearing an oversized white t-shirt.

Lola turned in Dre's direction.

"I'm leaving tomorrow," he told her.

Lola stopped brushing her hair long enough to give Dre her full undivided attention. "You're leaving?" she repeated.

Dre expected to hear a bit of relief in her tone, but instead heard a hint of disappointment. "Yeah," he said. "That's what you wanted, right?" he asked. "For me to get out ya hair...?"

Lola turned back towards the mirror and resumed brushing through her mane. "That is what I wanted...,"she whispered.

Dre raised an eyebrow in confusion. "Wanted?" he asked.

"I—I meant that's what I want," she stammered.

Dre slowly made his way inside her bedroom. With each step he took Lola's heart beat faster and harder. She then reflected back to the tense moment shared in the kitchen. Dre had the hairs on the nape of her standing up, and she, for the life of her, couldn't figure out why he was suddenly having this effect on her.

For goodness sakes the man had jumped into her car in the midst of oncoming traffic, threatened her life, and virtually held her hostage against her will...so why the hell was her body betraying her at that very moment?

Dre slowly stepped directly behind Lola. He was so close that she could feel his erection through the sweatpants he wore—that once belonged to Ricardo. He placed his arms on the dresser on either side of her body. She had nowhere to run. The hair on the nape of her neck quickly stood erect.

Dre gazed into Lola's eyes through the reflection in the dresser mirror. "What exactly do you want?" he asked in a low tone.

Lola slowly turned around to face him. She stared up into Dre's intense eyes, not bothering to respond immediately. Her full lips were slightly parted, her heart thumped rapidly in her chest...

Dre slowly leaned down and softly pressed his lips against hers. Lola quickly pulled away—which surprised him. He wasn't expecting that reaction at all. They silently gazed into one another's eyes as they tried to figure out what the other was thinking. Lola surprised herself and Dre when she suddenly pulled him down and crushed her lips against his.

His tongue eagerly slid inside her mouth. Lola slowly ran her fingers through Dre's mid-length dreadlocks. In a sudden swift movement, he hoisted her onto the dresser and slipped between her thighs. Their tongues wrestled passionately as they caressed each other in wantonness.

Lola didn't understand what exactly was happening, but she would be damned if she fought it.

Dre anxiously reached between her legs, slipped her panties to the side, and slipped two fingers inside her wet pussy.

"Ooohh," Lola moaned as she tossed her head back.

Dre bit his bottom lip, as he curved his fingers upward, and tickled her spot. Lola whimpered in response and leaned backward slightly. She moved her hips in a circular motion as she literally fucked Dre's fingers.

"This thing so damn tight, Lola," Dre whispered.

Her mouth widened, and her cheeks flushed. It had been so long since she had been touched in such a way.

Dre slowly withdrew his wet fingers and slicked the juices over Lola's swollen, throbbing clit. He massaged the sensitive flesh for several seconds, getting her even more sexually aroused, before sliding his fingers inside her mouth. She sucked passionately and eagerly, and the kinkiness he saw in her right then and there actually surprised him since she seemed so quiet, innocent, and soft-spoken.

After Lola had cleaned his fingers of any traces of her pussy juices, he lifted her up, and carried her over towards the queen-sized platform bed. They shared passionate kisses on the short trip there.

Once he carefully placed her down on the mattress, she hurriedly pulled her t-shirt over her head. To Dre's surprise she wasn't wearing a bra underneath. His mouth watered as he eyed her petite breasts and large, dark brown nipples.

Lola assisted Dre in removing his clothes. He pulled the sweatpants down his legs and she lifted his t-shirt over his head...The atmosphere in the room seemed to changed once she eyed the many bullet wound scars on his chest and abdomen.

An uncomfortable silence hung in the air as neither of them said a word. Dre was sure that she was probably turned off after seeing such a thing...but she actually surprised him when she slowly leaned down and began to place delicate kisses on each individual scar. Dre ran his both of his hands through her long, curly hair.

Lola sat upright and slipped her tongue inside his mouth. Dre savored the taste of her own juices on her tongue.

"Turn over," he said in a hoarse tone.

Lola gladly obliged as she turned in the opposite direction and positioned herself on her hands and knees. Dre slowly removed her panties and casually tossed them onto the floor. He positioned himself behind her and took his time as he guided the tip of his dick inside her wet and dripping pussy.

"*Aaaah,*" Lola moaned.

Dre decided to tease her a bit as he slid out of her, and then back inside but just a little bit farther that time.

Lola dropped her face into the plush cotton pillow to keep from screaming, but Dre grabbed a fistful of her hair and guided her back in position.

"Nuh-uh," Dre told her. "I want you just like this."

He slid farther inside, pulled out half-way, and then slammed back inside. Skin slapping and squelchy wet-noises were the only sounds perceivable in the bedroom. Lola grabbed a handful of the sheets as she fought to accept what Dre was giving to her.

"You takin' it like a pro," he said as he assaulted her pussy from the back. "This pussy so fuckin' tight. It's grippin' this dick too, ma."

Dre lifted his left leg and with one hand held onto her waist as he stroked faster, harder, and deeper. Lola helplessly dropped her face into the pillow, but Dre didn't mind as her ass remained upright. It was his favorite position. Face down, ass up.

"Shit," Dre groaned. "You finna have me cum all in this good ass pussy..." And he did shortly after.

Panting and trying to regain control of their breathing they lay next to one another staring up at the patterns on the ceiling.

Dre broke the silence. "I want to give you something before I go," he told Lola.

She turned on her side, propped her elbow up, and rested her head on her hand. "What's that?" she asked.

Dre slowly climbed out of bed, redressed, and left the bedroom. Several minutes later, he returned with the Glock 26 Maceo had given to him.

Lola instantly tensed up at the sight of the gun. "What the hell is that for?" she asked fearfully.

Dre sat on the edge of the mattress. "Protection," he told her.

"From what?" she asked irritated.

Dre turned and gave her a knowing look. "You don't want what I did to you to happen again. The next mothafucka may not be so nice," he said.

"I don't allow guns in my home," Lola said matter-of-factly.

"Look, I ain't tryin' to come up in here and fuck ya lil' program you got goin' on up, but the fact of the matter is, you need protection for you and Nina," Dre told her in an authoritative tone. "And what if that mothafucka comes back puttin' his hands on you?" he asked. "I won't be here to fuck him up."

Lola sighed deeply and looked down. She then reached over and placed a hand on Dre's toned thigh. "DeAndre," she said. "You don't have to leave..."

Dre couldn't believe what he was hearing. Just two days ago she had begged him to get the hell out of her home...now she was asking him to stay.

"I can't stay here, and you know that Lola," he told her.

"And why not?" she asked.

"Lola, I'm a wanted murderer," he told her. "I gotta get my black ass out the country."

She had a hopeful look in her eyes when she asked, "But you didn't do it, right?" she asked. "You're innocent."

Dre grimaced. "You must not have saw the footage on the news," he said. "I wish I can sit here and tell you I was innocent. I'm not gon' lie to ya ass about the dirt I did. I'm not that nigga, Lola."

Her cheeks flushed in embarrassment.

Dre slowly stood to his feet. He placed the Glock on her nightstand. "Put this up somewhere safe," he told her.

"I told you I don't allow guns in my home," she said. There was a hint of anger in her tone.

Her stubbornness reminded Dre of Nikki. His stomach instantly churned at the thought of Nikki as sadness swept over him. The most fucked up thing of all was not knowing if she had made it out of there alive or not. He assumed she had been killed, but he was not a hundred percent sure, and that's what really hurt.

"Do whatever you want with it, Lola," Dre said nonchalantly. "But I'm leaving it here," and with that said he left the bedroom and headed towards the living room.

Dre was surprised when Lola appeared in the living room ten minutes later. She had put the oversized t-shirt back on. She wore a look of irritation on her pretty face.

Dre looked up at Lola staring down at him with her arms folded. "You're right. You may not be innocent," she said. "I know you're not perfect...but there's good in you, DeAndre...I know there is. You're a good person—"

"I'm not no fuckin' good person," Dre cut her off. "You don't know me, Lola. You don't know shit about me. You don't know what I've done. You don't know what I'm capable of," he told her. "Because if you did, you wouldn't be sayin' this shit right now and you *damn* sure wouldn't have fucked me. So miss me with that therapist talk bullshit."

Lola was completely taken back by Dre's sudden change of attitude.

"I know what you doin'," Dre told her. "And I know what you thinkin', Lola. Look, I already put you in ya daughter in enough danger already. Feds bust in this bitch and they takin' ya ass to jail, and you'll never see Nina again. Lola, I ain't that nigga," he explained. "You need a good dude that's gon' take care of you and ya daughter and protect you. That's not me."

There was an uncomfortable silence between the two for several seconds.

"Am I supposed to be afraid now?" Lola asked. "The way you make it sound, I'm already in way too deep. Since you've risked my life, why not tell me who you *really* are?"

"Stop playin' wit me before I tell ya ass some shit you'd wish I hadn't. Just know that I ain't the nigga you think I am, and I ain't like none of these other niggas out here."

25

A tall, muscular, dark brown-skinned body guard drew his weapon and slowly approached the slightly ajar motel room door. After nudging the door open with the barrel of his gun, his eyes eagerly scanned the room.

The bed sheets were ruffled, used towels were scattered over the carpet, and a couple keycards were left on the nightstand. The motel room was vacant, but the fact that the room had yet to be cleaned informed the body guard that Nikki had recently left.

He lowered his gun and slowly exited the room. After returning to the Escalade, he climbed into the backseat, and closed the door behind himself.

"She wasn't there boss," he said.

Lexer sighed in frustration. He was surprisingly calm since he had expected Nikki to flee. Lexer pulled out his cellphone and dialed the number to his informant.

"Find her," Lexer said in a calm tone. "And find out whatever you can on the motherfucker that's helping her..."

***

Nikki seemed quieter than usual as she stared out the passenger window at the passing scenery. It was obvious that something was on her mind.

Maceo glanced in her direction. He then turned down the volume to the Meek Mill mixtape he was listening to. "You good ma?" he asked in a concerned tone.

Nikki slowly turned to face Maceo. He was shocked by what came out of her mouth.

"I don't want to have this baby," she admitted. "I want to get an abortion as soon as we get where we gotta go…"

Maceo didn't respond immediately as he absorbed her words. He really didn't like the talk of abortion. Especially not after the bomb Nadia had dropped on him.

There was an awkward silence between the two before he spoke again. "Would Dre want you to do that if he were alive?"

"No. But I'm sure he wouldn't want us fucking either," Nikki retorted. "And besides," she added. "The baby may not even be his…"

Maceo figured his ears had to be playing tricks on him. "Whatchu' mean the baby may not be his?" he asked. "Whose baby is it?"

Nikki was silent as she continued to stare out her window.

"I asked you whatchu' meant by that," he repeated in a stern voice.

No response.

Maceo shook his head in disbelief. "Damn, Nikki," he said. "You were fuckin' around on my boy? That's messed up."

Nikki quickly turned to face him. "You got a lot of damn nerve, Maceo. You don't know shit, aight? So don't sit here and pass judgment on something you have no idea about."

Maceo didn't respond as he continued to drive on 480.

***

Hassan had his duffle bag over his shoulder as he ran through a dark, damp alley. Nikki and Dre were fast on his heels. His heart pounded ferociously in his chest as he ran full speed—suddenly, he noticed he had run straight into a dead end.

"Ain't nowhere to run yo' punk ass to now!" Dre taunted him. His gun hung loosely at his side as he stared intently at his former best friend.

Hassan's eyes darted from Dre to Nikki. "So this is it?" he asked. "You gon' kill me? Fuck it. Do what you do."

A devilish grin crept across Dre's lips. "Nah. I ain't gon' kill you," he said. Dre handed the gun to Nikki. "She is..."

Hassan's expression softened as he stared at Nikki.

"Shoot him right between his mothafuckin' eyes," Dre coached her.

Nikki aimed the gun at Hassan, but hesitated to pull the trigger.

"Shoot this nigga!" Dre barked.

Nikki shuffled about uncomfortably. Evidently, she was having difficulty pulling the trigger on the man she once considered to be her best friend.

"What are you waitin' on?! Shoot this mothafucka!"

"I can't!" Nikki bellowed. Tears streamed from her eyes as she slowly lowered the weapon.

Dre was enraged. "Fuck it." He snatched the gun from Nikki and stood in front of her. "I'll do it."

Hassan suddenly snatched his gun out and aimed it at Dre!

POP!

Dre ducked in the nick of time, avoiding death by milliseconds. Nikki, on the other hand, wasn't so fortunate. Hassan's bullet struck her directly in the forehead and inch above her left eyebrow.

She seemingly fell backwards in slow motion and landed with a thud on the cold, concrete.

Dre's eyes widened in shock and disbelief. "Nikki?!" He kneeled down beside her. "You mothafucka!" he screamed.

Dre carefully pulled Nikki into his arms and held her motionless body. Tears slipped from his eyes as he rocked her in his strong embrace.

Suddenly, he felt the barrel of a gun pressed firmly against the back of his head. Dre slowly closed his eyes, and accepted his fate.

POP!

...Dre quickly sat upright on the floral living room sofa. He was panting and sweating profusely. The nightmare he had just experienced felt so vivid and frighteningly realistic.

His eyes scanned the dark room, and he slowly relaxed. Dre knew he would not be able to sleep peacefully again until he located Hassan, and put a bullet in his dome.

***

The following morning, Lola wasn't hiding the fact that she was slightly irritated about Dre's departure. She watched as he pulled on a pair of New Balances—tennis shoes that once belonged to Ricardo.

Dre then stood to his feet, and walked over to Lola. Her arms were folded and she had a disapproving expression on her face.

Dre leaned down and attempted to plant an innocent kiss on her forehead, but she quickly moved her face away. The gesture hurt his feelings a tad bit, but he took it for what it was.

"You stay up, aight?" he said before walking out the front door.

Dre had made it to the bottom of the porch steps when Lola suddenly appeared in the doorway. He turned and looked at her. She hesitated as she tried to find the right words to say.

"DeAndre...," she began. "Just...um...just be careful...okay?"

"I'll try," he said nonchalantly. "But I ain't gon' make any promises..."

26

Every second, every minute…

Man I swear that she can get it…

Say if you a bad bitch, put ya hands up high…

Hands up high…hands up high…

Hassan had touched down in the US a couple hours earlier. Barcelona was gorgeous, and everything he had envisioned and more, but quite frankly he missed his city. It didn't take long at all for the homesickness to kick in.

The first place he went was Secrets Gentlemen's located on the west side of Cleveland. He was never really a fan of strip clubs, but Secrets was not very far from the airport, and Hassan could use a drink as well as some paid for female companionship.

Secrets had the baddest females Cleveland had to offer. They came in a variety of colors, shapes, and sizes, but the one thing they all shared in common was beauty.

Kendrick Lamar's "*Poetic Justice*" was playing on maximum volume throughout the popular strip club.

Hassan took a seat at the bar. "Let me get a double of Patron and a Corona," he ordered.

From the corner of his eye, he noticed a female approaching. “Hey, babe. You want some some company?”

Hassan was just about to tell the female that he had not even gotten settled in until he turned and took in her appearance. She definitely looked like the type of a woman a nigga would have a hard time saying ‘no’ to…and for damn good reasons. She was bad and she knew it.

“Damn,” Hassan said taking in her appearance. “Let me think about it. Turn around let me see what you workin’ with,” he told her.

Nadia tossed her long, jet black hair over her shoulder, and slowly spun around so that Hassan could take in her physique. She wore a hot pink bikini style slingshot. A pair of tiny, hot pink boy shorts covered her huge ass.

“Damn, girl. Your ass should be in Atlanta somewhere, shouldn’t you,” Hassan teased. “Hell yeah you can keep me company. What you drinkin’ on?”

“I’ll have a shot of whatever you’re drinking on,” she said.

Hassan gestured to the bartender to pour another shot of Patron. “So what’s your name?” he asked.

“Nadia,” she smiled.

I really hope you play this…

'Cause ole' girl you test my patience...

"You bad then a mothafucka, but I know I ain't tellin' you shit you ain't already heard," Hassan said. "Yo, why don't on the next song you give me a lap dance?"

"I can do that," she smiled.

"In the VIP room," Hassan added.

Nadia beamed. "I can do that too." She instantly perked up at the mention of VIP room. Only the real ballers could afford to go upstairs to the luxurious VIP room. Lap dances also cost twenty dollars per dance.

"Show me the way then," he told her.

***

I don't wanna give you the wrong impression...

I need love and affection...

And I hope I'm not sounding too desperate...

I need love and affection...

Hassan watched as Nadia seductively removed her boy shorts and tossed them onto the carpet. She then removed the straps that were covering her large, perky breasts. Hassan nodded his head in approval at the sight of her nipple rings. Before the night ended, he was determined to fuck her.

Hassan tossed a stack of singles at her. "Let me see that ass," he told her.

Nadia slowly turned around, and began swaying seductively to the mellow beat of the song.

Love...

Love...

Love...

Love and affection...

Hassan gently squeezed on one of her massive butt cheeks.

"You know you aren't supposed to touch," Nadia teased.

Hassan grinned. "Shit we're back here all alone," he told her. "The curtains drawn. Ain't no video cameras. We can do whatever the fuck we wanna do," he hinted.

Nadia smirked at his comment. "You're something else," she told him.

Hassan was just about to squeeze on her other butt cheek until suddenly something caught his attention. Written in bold, cursive lettering on her cheek was the words: Property of Maceo.

His eyebrows furrowed in confusion.

Maceo.

There weren't too many niggas with the name Maceo...especially in Cleveland. *I know this ain't Maceo's old lady,* Hassan said to himself.

"You got a nigga?" Hassan asked Nadia.

Nadia turned around and climbed into Hassan's lap. "Should I have one?" she asked flirtatiously.

"Well, I peeped ya tat. That's why I'm asking."

Nadia frowned. "Oh...that..."

"Let me ask you somethin'," Hassan began. "Your nigga Maceo wouldn't be the same one that sell guns and shit, would it?"

"First of all, he's not man," she corrected him. "As a matter of fact, I'm getting that shit covered ASAP. Nigga ran off with some slanted eyed bitch named Nikki..."

Hassan's ears instantly perked up at the mention of Nikki's name. "Nikki?" he repeated. "She's really short? Brown-skinned? Kinda petite?"

Nadia snorted. "Yeah that's that hoe..."

"You don't know where they're at now, do you?" Hassan eagerly asked.

Nadia sucked her teeth. "Why're you asking all these damn questions?"

Hassan brandished a couple hundred dollar bills before placing them into her garter belt.

"I caught their asses together at the Kirkland Inn Motel. That was a few days ago though. Last I heard, he was takin' this bitch to Mexico or some shit—"

"Mexico?"

"That's what I said," Nadia confirmed.

Hassan sat speechless as he absorbed her words. *Well, I'll be damned*, Hassan told himself.

Rihanna and Future's "*Love Song*" ended and now Rihanna's "Cockiness" was blaring through the speakers.

"Do you want another dance?" Nadia asked snapping Hassan from his profound thoughts.

"Nah," he declined.

Nadia began to stand up, but Hassan firmly stopped her from moving.

"I wanna know how much it costs," he told her.

"I don't turn tricks," she said matter-of-factly.

"I bet you will for the right price," Hassan challenged.

"I bet I don't," Nadia said finality.

***

"*Aaahh*! Fuck me!" Nadia screamed as she held firmly onto the headboard.

Hassan slapped her round ass as he fiercely hit it from the back. “Don’t run from it,” he demanded.

“Oooohh, shit!” Nadia whimpered.

Singles littered the carpet of the motel room as well as the queen size bed. Nadia had put on a little private show, but eventually Hassan was tired of the entertainment and teasing. He wanted to hit it, and get back to business.

Hassan grabbed a handful of Nadia’s jet black hair, and gripped her shoulder, as he slammed his pelvis against her ass.

She inched away a little unable to handle his powerful strokes.

Hassan firmly held her in place. “All this ass…you better take this dick,” he said. “Throw that shit back.”

Nadia’s cheeks flushed and turned a bright pink color. Her breasts swung with each powerful stroke Hassan inflicted. She attempted to match his harsh strokes as she tossed it back onto his lengthy pole.

“Fuck! Shit! I’m ‘bout to cum,” she announced.

“Come on this dick,” Hassan told her. “I want you to cum all over it…”

“*Aaaahhh*!” Nadia cried out. “Damn!”

28

"Damn," Nikki shuffled in her seat. "How much longer we got?" she asked.

"Not too much longer," Maceo told her.

"Have you been here before?" Nikki asked. "To Oaxaca? What made you pick this city?"

Maceo chuckled. He had this faraway look in his eyes as he drove. "My pops used to bring me and moms here every summer when I was a kid. Me, personally, I loved the coast. But pops…he loved the cultures. He was into shit like that."

Nikki looked over at him. "You ever plan on taking your daughter here someday?" she asked.

Maceo shrugged. "Maybe," he said. "Someday…"

***

Hassan took a swig from his Corona. His eyes were fastened to the sports channel on the TV bar inside The Spot II however his mind was elsewhere. He could not stop thinking about what Nadia had told him.

"Aye, man…how ya brother holdin' up?" A guy Hassan only recognized from the hood approached him. "I heard that nigga was fighting for his life in the hospital," he said. "Damn shame…"

Hassan was completely at a lost to what the guy was saying. He had put a bullet in Careem's head over a month ago. Careem couldn't possibly be alive. *Could he,* Hassan wondered. He had pretty much left his brother for dead, but it wasn't as if he had checked his pulse either.

"The hell you talkin' b....," Hassan voice trailed off as his heart instantly sank to the pit of his stomach. He felt as if he were literally looking at ghost! No! It couldn't be!

Hassan sat frozen in place, as Dre stared directly at him from the doorway of the small bar. The fact that both men were at the same place at the same time was pure coincidence.

No one else in the bar seemed to notice or care about the sudden tension that filled the room. Curren$y's *"Jet Life Remix"* blared through the speakers of the bar. Most men were sipping and chilling. Some were trying to run game on the few females there. Everyone was pretty much preoccupied. Yet Dre and Hassan stood motionless as they stared into each other's cold eyes.

Don't miss this jet hoe...

Don't miss this jet hoe...

Talkin' jet life to the next life...

Jet life to the next life...

Suddenly, and without warning, Dre took off running towards Hassan!

Hassan quickly hopped off his barstool nearly tripping in the process. In a desperate attempt to defend himself, he launched the Corona he had previously been sipping on at Dre's head.

Dre ducked in the nick of time! The glass bottle connected with an innocent bystander's back.

"Fuck you runnin' for nigga?!" Dre yelled. He shoved people out of his way, and knocked barstools over as he raced towards Hassan who quickly took refuge on the side of the bar.

"Fuck you!" Hassan shouted before snatching his pistol out.

POP!

POP!

He recklessly aimed shots in Dre's direction.

Women screamed in fear, and people hurriedly raced to get out of the club. Hassan's bullets accidentally clipped the guy who he had previously been talking to. The guy helplessly dropped onto the floor, and was painfully trampled over by everyone rushing to get out of the club.

Women's heels poked into his back, and the weight of everyone stepping onto him, crushed his ribcage.

"Aaargghh!" He cried out in pain as his ribs broke and pierced organs causing internal bleeding.

Dre grabbed the nearest bar stool, and launched it in Hassan's direction. "You thought I was dead, huh, nigga?!" he screamed like a madman.

The chair flew into the wall behind Hassan. He quickly scrambled to his feet and darted towards the back of the club.

Dre attempted to pursue him, but with everyone running in the opposite direction, the task was extremely hard and he eventually lost sight of Hassan.

Hassan tore through the back door, and raced through the alley. He knew the shortcuts like the back of his hand, and expertly navigated through the alley and backyards as if he were following a map.

Hassan did not stop running until he knew for sure that he was no longer being pursued. He kneeled over and placed his hands on his knees as he fought to gain control of his breathing. In the distance he could hear the resonance of ambulance and police sirens approaching.

***

"Put your fucking hands in the air!" A cop barked at Dre. His weapon was aimed, and he had no hesitation to fire if need be.

Dre stared at the gun clutched tightly in the officer's grip. He weighed his options although the only ones he had were life and death. He could surrender and be taken in by the authorities or he could force them to have to shoot him where he stood.

Dre cringed inwardly at the thought of prison. To be honest, he would prefer death. It wasn't as if he could cop a plea bargain in his case. He was fucked.

Suddenly, Dre turned on his heel and attempted to run out the same back door Hassan had torn through only minutes earlier.

POP!

A bullet tore through his calf muscle instantly stopping him in his tracks. Dre slowly crashed down onto the bar's sticky floor that was partially covered in shattered glass—from where people had dropped their drinks before fleeing from the bar. Lying motionless a few feet from where he lay was the guy who had been trampled over. His eyes were wide open and glazed over. Blood seeped from his parted lips and created a small puddle near his face.

"Put your hands behind your head!"

Dre peeled his cheek off the sticky floor and glanced at the few people—that were still inside the bar—watching him get arrested.

"I said put your hands behind your head!" the police officer yelled.

Dre reluctantly did as he was told.

Several police officers quickly rushed over to apprehend him.

29

Even with everything that had just happened with Dre at the bar, Hassan had to know if Careem was still alive in the hospital fighting to survive. He had to see it for himself, because right now it just didn't seem believable.

After retrieving his vehicle, he raced to the nearest hospital which was Southpointe—the same hospital he had been rushed to after being shot. Once he made it to the front information desk, he was informed that no one by the name of Careem Bashir was currently a patient.

Maybe he had his facts fucked up, Hassan told himself. Even though he tried to convince himself that Careem was dead, he still ended up driving to Metro Hospital on the west side of Cleveland. Hassan would not be full convinced until he knew for sure.

He took a final puff on the Black N' Mild he was smoking, and stepped out of his car. After tossing the butt, he headed towards the Metro Hospital entrance.

A pudgy Hispanic female employee sat behind the information desk in the lobby.

"Hello. Good evening," Hassan greeted with a fabricated smile. "I'm here to see my brother."

She frowned. "I'm sorry," she apologized. "But visiting hours ended an hour ago."

Hassan sighed in disappointment. “Really? Wow,” he said. “And I flew all the way here to see him. My flight ended up getting delayed and—”

“You know what,” she cut him off. “I’ll see what I can do for you. What’s his name?”

A sneaky smirk crept across Hassan’s lips, but the employee’s eyes were too busy planted to the screen of her computer to notice.

“Careem Bashir.”

Her fingers clacked away on the computer’s keyboard as she tried to locate his brother in the system.

“Says here, he’s in ICU,” she told Hassan.

Well, I’ll be damned, he thought to himself. *This mothafucka really is alive.*

***

Boop.

Boop.

Boop.

The consistent beeps from Careem’s respiratory heart monitor were the only sounds perceivable in his hospital room. Hassan slowly made his way towards his brother and took in his appearance. His stomach churned as he took slow steps towards Careem.

It was obvious that his older brother was fighting for his life, but the damage done was not caused by his hands.

Hassan wore a disturbed expression as he eyed the burnt, pink flesh that covered over seventy-five percent of Careem's body. If it had not been for the nurse directing Hassan to this exact room, he would have never believed that the gruesome, decrepit figure in the hospital bed was Careem.

"Damn, bro...," Hassan whispered. "The fuck happened...?" He stared down into his brother's burnt, disfigured face. "Bet you wish that bullet'd killed ya ass now..."

Careem slowly cracked his right eye open. His lips parted as if he were readying to say something but nothing came out.

For a split second, Hassan actually felt sympathy and compassion for his older brother—but the sentiment immediately faded. Without warning, he slowly slipped the plush pillow from beneath Careem's bandaged head, and held it firmly in his hand. He then glanced over his shoulder. The door was slightly ajar, but there were no passing nurses.

Hassan looked down at Careem. He had closed his eye...almost as if he were accepting his fate with dignity.

"Don't worry, bruh," Hassan said. "I'm finna put ya ass out ya misery..."

Hassan slowly lifted the pillow—

"Aww, how nice of you. Fluffing the pillow for him," a cheerful voice stated.

Hassan quickly turned around, and stared at the young, Caucasian nurse that had just entered the room.

"Is that your brother?" she asked.

Hassan pretended to fluff the pillow, and slowly repositioned it underneath Careem's head. "Yep. My big bro'..." He tried his best to sound disappointed and unnerved.

"Well, I won't be here too long," she explained. "I just need to check his vital signs, and then I'll be out of your hair."

Hassan remained patient, and allowed the nurse to do her thing. Once her duty was complete, she quickly left the room, politely closing the door behind herself.

Hassan stared down at Careem in disgust for several seconds. He then leaned down towards his brother, and whispered, "You know what? You deserve to sit ya ass here and suffer..."

Careem's eyelids fluttered in response. He couldn't physically speak, but if he could he would've begged Hassan to end his pain and suffering.

"...And that's just what I'ma let you do..." Hassan turned on his heel and left the room.

***

Two days later, Nikki stepped onto the wrap around balcony of her two-story home. She had purchased the house a day after they made it into Oaxaca. The fully furnished three bedroom three bathroom was complimented by a beautiful garden, and array of tropical trees. Nikki was granted a view of the four feet deep plunge pool in her backyard.

"I can't believe it," she told herself. "I'm here. I really made it..."

Maceo suddenly stepped through the French doors of the bedroom that led onto the balcony. He was shirtless, barefoot, and only wore a pair of Pajama pants. Nikki continued to stare out at the view. It was absolutely breath-taking, especially at night.

Maceo slowly stepped behind Nikki, and placed his hands on the railing on either side of her body. He then bent down and kissed the side of her head.

"You know I have to leave soon...," he whispered.

Nikki slowly turned around and faced him. She stared up into his big, brown eyes. "When are you leaving?" she asked in a soft tone.

"I need to be gettin' on the road tomorrow," he explained.

Nikki looked disappointed as her gaze dropped to the floor.

Maceo lifted her chin upward. "You good?" he asked in a concerned tone.

"I don't wanna be alone," she whispered.

"Nikki, you know you ain't alone. I'ma be here for you every step of the way through the pregnancy and everything," he added. "I'm all the way in—"

"Then stay here," Nikki interrupted. "Stay here…with me…"

Maceo sighed. "You know I got my hustle," he told her. "And my baby girl in Cleveland. I can't just stay here…even though it does sound temptin'…but I gotta get back to the grind. You know I'm comin' back as often as I can—"

"But I love you," Nikki suddenly admitted.

Maceo sighed dejectedly, and looked away avoiding her intense stare. Nikki searched his face, patiently waiting for a response.

He looked down at his bare feet, and then back at Nikki. "You don't love me, Nikki—"

"How are you gonna tell me what I feel," she argued.

"I'm not him. I told ya ass in the beginning not to get ya feelin' caught up with a nigga like me—"

"Yeah, I know what you told me," she cut him off. "But I ain't thinking about that shit. And besides it's too late. I already fell, and you warning me wasn't gonna to stop it from happening," Nikki said. "Look, I'm not asking you to marry me, Maceo…I just wanted you to know how I felt." With that said Nikki walked around him, and headed towards the bedroom.

Maceo suddenly grabbed Nikki's forearm, stopping her in her tracks. He slowly pulled her close to him.

Their bodies were firmly pressed against each other's. She looked up into his face as he stared down into her hazel eyes. Maceo slowly framed her face with his hands before leaning down to kiss her. He passionately nibbled and sucked on her bottom lip.

The bright full moon looked beautiful in the pitch black sky.

Maceo carefully lifted Nikki into his arms and carried her towards the bedroom.

***

Lexer answered his cellphone on the first ring. Time was of the essence, and it had already been wasted trying to track Nikki down. He could not wait to get his hands on her. Whether he got the money back or not, he was going to make her suffer badly for ever underestimating him.

Lexer was not a game, and he did not appreciate being treated as such. Frankly, he felt as if it he had let her off way too easily, but he would be damned if he made the same mistake twice.

"I hope you have good news," Lexer said.

His informant hesitated. "Well…I'm doing everything I can, but I can no longer locate Nikita Brown. Honestly, she may have just changed her name…I'm not quite sure, but I'm looking into it," he explained in a nervous tone. "I *did* however pull up some information on a Maceo Valentino," he said. "In 2008, Nikita was arrested on robbery charges. The weapon she used was traced back to him. He could be our guy, boss. He could be the one that's helping her."

"Find out everything you can on him," Lexer said. "These motherfuckers are going to learn I'm not the one to fuck with."

30

THREE DASYS LATER

Maceo was guided down a narrow hallway that led to the jail's inmate visitation room. He was then instructed by a correction officer to have a seat in the empty booth. Dre sat on the opposite side of the glass partition which was separating them.

He wore a grim expression on his face as he patiently waited for Maceo to pick up the telephone receiver.

"What's up, man?" Maceo greeted. "I got here as soon as I heard. The hell happened, Dre?"

Dre shook his head and sighed. "Hell, I'm still tryin' to figure that shit out myself," he said.

"Did you go to court yet?" Maceo asked.

"Tomorrow, bruh," Dre answered.

"Damn," Maceo sighed. "Shit's fucked up."

"Nah, what's most fucked up is I ain't even get a chance to murk this nigga for what he did to Nikki," Dre said. "I mean the shit was this fuckin' close." He held up his index finger and thumb. "Real talk, I wasted too much fuckin' time when I should've been lookin' for this nigga." Dre shook his head and ran a hand through his dreadlocks. "All the shit I did was for nothin'. I'm right where the fuck I said I'd never end back up...Nikki's dead...and right now I just wish this nigga Hassan had killed my ass too."

Maceo scratched his beard as he stared at his homie through the glass partition. He had allowed Nikki to continue believing Dre was dead, and Dre to believe Nikki was dead. He was playing the fence, but he felt that now was as good as time as any to finally tell Dre the truth.

"Nikki, ain't dead, man..."

Dre slowly looked at Maceo. He didn't respond immediately. "I must not have heard you, bruh. Say what now?" he asked.

"Nikki...she ain't dead..."

Dre was obviously taken aback by what he was hearing. "The fuck you mean she ain't dead?"

"Nigga, you said yaself you ain't see Hassan kill her," Maceo noted. "So I'm just here to tell you, she ain't dead."

"You know where Nikki is? You've seen her?" Dre eagerly asked.

Maceo didn't respond.

"Where is she?!" Dre demanded to know.

"You don't need to know all that my nigga," Maceo said nonchalantly. "Just know she's alive...and safe," he added.

"I don't need to know—nigga, you straight trippin'! You better tell me where the fuck my girl is!" Dre barked.

Maceo was totally unfazed by Dre's temperament. "Like I said, you don't need to know. Just be grateful I told ya ass so you don't have to sit in jail for life wonderin'," he said coolly.

"What?! Bitch nigga, I'll kill yo' ass!" Dre yelled. "Tell me where the fuck she is right now!"

"She's better off without ya mothafuckin' ass," Maceo said in a calm tone before politely hanging up the phone.

In a sudden fit of rage, Dre began to pound on the glass with the telephone receiver. "You been fuckin' her?!" he screamed. "Nigga you ain't shit! *I'ma kill yo' mothafuckin' ass*!"

Maceo stood from his seat and slowly exited the room. He said all he had to say.

Dre continued to assault the glass partition as he tossed out meaningless threats. Seconds later, he was finally escorted out the visitation room by correction officers.

***

Maceo headed straight to his baby mama's house after the brief visitation with Dre. He wanted to spend a little time with his daughter Kay, and hopefully slide up in Quita if she acted right. However, the moment he reached her unit, he noticed something was obviously wrong. Her apartment door was slightly ajar.

Maceo grabbed his piece and slowly entered the apartment. "Quita?" he called out.

"*Maceo, help*!"

Maceo quickly ran in the direction of the living room, and suddenly stopped in his tracks at the scene before him.

Quita sat on one sofa while MaKayla sat on the opposite one crying. Several armed men stood in the living room with their guns aimed at Maceo. They were ready for him to make the wrong move.

Lexer sat beside Quita with one leg folded over the other. He looked more like an invited guest than someone that was holding a family hostage.

"I take it you must be Maceo," Lexer said in a deep, baritone voice. A devilish smirk tugged at his lips, but there was no trace of humor in his eyes. "We were just talking about you." He seductively trailed the suppressor of the Beretta 9mm along Quita's face.

"The fuck ya'll want man?!" Maceo asked. "If this is some shit got to do with me, then let my family go."

"You are not in the position right now to compromise," Lexer said. "Drop your gun."

Maceo's nostrils flared wildly. His heart beat rapidly in his chest. He weighed his options but quickly realized he had none.

Lexer cocked the hammer and placed the 9mm to Quita's temple. She instantly tensed up in fear as tears streamed down her cheeks. Her eyes pleaded with Maceo to do as he was told.

"I said drop the fucking gun," Lexer repeated in a calm tone.

Maceo reluctantly did as he was told.

Lexer slowly lowered the gun from Quita's head. "You know Maceo," he began. "You wouldn't even be involved in all this right now...if you had just minded your fucking business. Now I'm only going to ask once," he said. "Where is that bitch?"

Maceo tried to stall. "Who?" he asked.

"Maceo, please! Just tell him where the hell Nikki is! This bitch ain't worth all of us dying for!" Quita screamed. She would have gladly blurted out Nikki's location if she could remember the unique name of the city Maceo had told her.

Lexer smiled and nodded his head in agreement. "Listen to her," he said. "She's a smart woman."

"Look, I don't know where the fuck she's at, aight?"

Lexer sighed in frustration, and shook his head. Without warning, he fired a single shot that landed in Quita's chest.

PFEW!

MaKayla screamed!

Quita slowly rolled off the couch clutching her chest before tumbling to the plush carpeted floor.

"*Mothafucka*!" Maceo screamed.

"You're making this more difficult than it has to be!" Lexer yelled. His deep voice bounced off the living room's walls.

Maceo watched as Quita's chest slowly heaved up and down until it finally stopped once and for all. A pool of blood slowly formed around her body.

Lexer pointed the gun at Maceo.

"I ain't tellin you shit nigga!" Maceo yelled. "You think this the first time I ever had a mothafuckin' gun pointed in my face?!"

"No. I don't," Lexer said. "But it surely can be your last."

"Fuck you!" Maceo spat.

"Well…I gave you a chance…"

PFEW!

PFEW!

Two bullets tore through Maceo's torso!

MaKayla was crying hysterically at that point.

Maceo slowly dropped to his knees, and fell over.

"We're done here," Lexer said before standing to his feet.

His body guards led the way out the apartment. As Lexer passed Maceo's body, he looked down at him and shook his head. "I guess she was worth dying for," Lexer said before firing another shot in Maceo's back.

Maceo cringed in pain after the gunshot.

"*Mommy*?!" MaKayla cried. "*Daddy*?!" She hurriedly scrambled down from the couch once Lexer and his posse left.

Maceo slowly crawled over towards his daughter. He coughed up a mouthful of thick blood that oozed down his chin. "It's alright, Kay...," he whispered.

MaKayla stared at her mother's motionless body.

Maceo continued to crawl closer to his child, leaving a blood trail behind. "MaKayla..." He was only two feet away from her when he suddenly collapsed.

31

TEN MONTHS LATER

Nikki was maintaining good on her own. She had landed a job position teaching English as a second language at a school located in the center of Oaxaca. She had given birth to a healthy little boy five weeks ago, and life was good...but best of all it was normal.

Nikki wasn't as hurt as she thought she would be when Maceo hadn't contacted her again. To be honest, she saw it coming. And maybe it was even for the best. Nikki was kidding herself. Instead of leaving her heart at the door she had worn it proudly on her sleeve.

However, Nikki wasn't bitter about the situation at all. She was grateful for everything Maceo had done for her...including talking her out of getting the abortion. She would forever be grateful for that.

Alita, Nikki's full time nanny, prepared dinner while Nikki tended to her son upstairs. Alita's primary responsibility was to take care of the infant when Nikki was at work, but she also did other household duties such as cooking, doing laundry, and light housework. She took a load off Nikki who of course was new to the world of motherhood.

Nikki slowly walked around the room as she held her son and soothingly rubbed his back. Being a mother wasn't as bad as she thought. Actually it was pretty amazing. The very first time she held her son, she felt love, warmth, and tender kindness. Sentiments she had never fully experienced until motherhood.

Nikki slowly placed her sleeping child into his crib. He was an exact replica of his dad. From the curly hair, to the skin tone, to the light brown eyes. Hayden Bashir looked every bit like Hassan.

Nikki leaned down and placed a soft kiss on his forehead, before quietly leaving the bedroom.

Downstairs Alita was test-tasting the pasta sauce. She was completely unaware of the suspicious vehicle that had just pulled up to Nikki's home.

Nikki slowly made her way down the stairs—

BOOM!

The front door flew off the hinges as several husky men stormed inside!

Nikki instantly stopped in her tracks.

Alita dropped the wooden spoon she was holding, and rushed into the foyer to investigate the noise.

Tat! *Tat*! *Tat*! *Tat*! *Tat*! *Tat*! *Tat*!

Alita's body was riddled with bullets from an Mp5 submachine gun!

Nikki quickly took off running up the stairs at the sound of the loud gunshots. She tripped and stumbled every few stairs. Her heart hammered in her chest as she feared the worse.

Lexer slowly stepped inside the home. He took one look at the dead nanny lying sprawled out on the floor and frowned.

Tracking down Nikki had been no easy task. However, he had finally located her after months of grueling searching. Lexer was determined to make Nikki pay. She had fucked up by underestimating what he was capable of.

Nikki raced up the lengthy flight of stairs and ran towards her son's bedroom.

Lexer pulled out his gun, stepped over the nanny's lifeless body, and slowly made his way up the stairs.

He motioned to his body guards to search the home.

Nikki ran inside Hayden's bedroom, slammed the door shut, and locked it. Not fully content, she quickly pushed the Camden light dresser in front of the door.

Panting and sweating profusely, Nikki stared at the closed door for several seconds.

BOOM!

Nikki flinched and screamed at the sudden pounding on the closed bedroom door. Hayden suddenly began wailing.

One of Lexer's body guards rammed his shoulder into the bedroom door as Lexer stood nearby patiently waiting for entrance.

"Leave me the fuck alone!" Nikki screamed in fear.

"You should have known I would find you!" Lexer told her. "I told you don't fuck with me!"

BOOM!

The body guard slammed into the door again. The dresser holding the door closed moved slightly, but the door remained closed.

Nikki quickly ran over to Hayden, and picked him up. She held her son close as she watched the dresser move a few more inches.

Tears streamed from her eyes. *This shit is not happening*! *This shit is not happening*, she kept telling herself. But it was...she was finally coming face to face with her worst nightmare...

PART THREE IS NOW AVAILABLE! VISIT AMAZON.COM

EXCLUSIVE EXCERPT FROM "EBONY AND IVORY"

Ebony quickly snatched the sheets off of her and started to hop out the bed until Mario stepped into the bedroom carrying a glass of ice filled water.

"What happened?" Ebony asked slightly alarmed but nevertheless relieved.

"Somebody parked across the street and left their damn lights on."

Damn Ivory, how simpleminded can you be, Ebony asked herself.

He eyeballed Ebony suspiciously. "And where you 'bout to go? I ain't done with you. Shit, I want my money's worth," he told her before placing the glass of water on the night table.

Ebony rolled her eyes and sighed inwardly as Mario slipped his erect dick through the opening of his Hanes boxers. She didn't anticipate for their "session" to last this long and she damn sure didn't anticipate that it'd take Ivory twice as long to locate Mario's safe. Ebony was sure that he had some type of stash in his house. Hell, most dope boys did. And he clearly stated that he didn't have a bank account so where else would his money be? She hoped like hell that she didn't set herself up on a dummy mission and that it was indeed money in here to begin with.

Mario stood at the edge of the bed between Ebony's legs and softly guided her head in the direction of his loins. Through her peripheral vision, she clearly noticed Ivory creep into the bedroom. Ebony's eyes quickly shot open in their sockets. All Mario had to do was look over his shoulder and see her sister standing right there, intruding as clear as day.

What the hell is she doing, Ebony asked herself.

Ivory slowly took steps towards the master bathroom, careful not to cause any creaking sounds in the cherry hardwood floors. She stopped halfway and mouthed the words: I didn't see anything.

"Mmm, baby. That feels so good," Mario moaned. "You gon' catch this nut in yo' mouth?" he asked. "You gon' swallow it baby?"

Ivory waved her hands frantically as she silently panicked. As quietly as she could, she tiptoed into the master bathroom and disappeared out of sight.

"You gon' catch this nut?" Mario repeated.

"Mmmhmm," Ebony hesitantly agreed in a muffled voice.

"Here it comes," he told her.

Ebony closed her eyes tightly and reluctantly accepted the bitter tasting load Mario had to offer.

"Oh, baby," Mario said breathlessly. "You the fuckin' best." He slowly pulled his now flaccid penis from her mouth and plopped down on the edge of the bed with his back facing her.

Ebony didn't miss this opportunity to spit the mouthful of nut into his glass of ice cold water. She smiled devilishly as she swished the contents around in the glass. Drink up motherfucker, she thought to herself.

"I gotta take a piss," he suddenly said standing to his feet.

Ebony's eyes shot open in fear as she watched Mario make his way towards the master bathroom. Her lips parted as she tried to think of something to say...unfortunately nothing came to mind. Her heart suddenly dropped into the pit of her stomach at the sound of his urine splashing into the water of the toilet. This isn't happening!

Mario reclined his head as he allowed nature to take its course...Suddenly, the sound of movement startled him. He assumed Ebony had just come into the bathroom behind him. The minute he turned and looked behind himself, he flinched at the unexpected sight of the woman standing beside the doorframe with her back pressed against the wall. He had walked right past her and not even noticed her. Subconsciously, he released his dick and his urine spilled onto the toilet seat before spraying the white tile surrounding his feet.

"What the...fuck?" Mario looked to Ivory then back at Ebony who was sitting up in bed with the sheets nestled tightly around her bosom. Their expressions matched, and it wasn't simply because they were identical twins. They were in cahoots with one another! It took Mario less than two seconds to realize what was going on. "You bitches tryin' to rob me?!"

There was a tense moment of silence before anyone spoke again. Ebony's heart beat rapidly as her fists clutched the plush sheets. Ivory's chest heaved up and down slowly as she took uneven breaths. Her eyes darted in every direction but she refused to look at Mario.

I knew I shouldn't have let Ebony's ass talk me into this shit, Ivory thought. If we make it out of here, I will never do anything like this again, she promised herself.

Ebony was the first to break the nerve-racking silence. "M Mario," she stuttered. "Let me explain..."

Ivory however wasn't trying to explain a damn thing. She just wanted to get out of this situation by any means necessary. In a sudden state of panic and fear she darted towards the bathroom door in order to flee—

Yet Mario's fist instantly caught hold of her quick weave, halting her in her tracks.

"Aaahh!" she cried out in pain.

Her tear ducts stung as she felt small strands of her real hair being torn from her scalp underneath the quick weave. If she could, she would have gladly taken off running, leaving the eighteen inch weave in his tight grip. Yet the fresh quick weave was done far too tightly to permit her escape.

"And where the fuck you think you goin' hoe?!" he sneered.

Ebony quickly jumped out the bed butt ass naked at the exact same moment that Mario slammed Ivory's skull against the doorframe.

"Don't touch her motherfucker!" Ebony screamed. Spittle flew from her mouth as she yelled and charged at him full speed.

Ivory's limp body went crashing into the bathroom tile. Ebony was unsure if she was either conscious or out cold. Cocking her fist back, she ran towards Mario and took an uncoordinated swing towards his head.

He quickly and effortlessly ducked her futile blow before sending a vicious slap across her left cheek. Ebony went flying backwards before falling against the bathroom's marble wall. Her head collided with the wall upon impact and she uncontrollably slid down onto the floor. Dark red blood leaked from the split in her bottom lip, dripping down her chin.

"Ya'll hoes got the right one!" he yelled cockily.

NOW AVAILABLE! VISIT AMAZON.COM

ABOUT THE AUTHOR

Jade Jones discovered her passion for creative writing in elementary school. Born in 1989, she began writing short stories and poetry as an outlet. Later on, as a teen, she led a troubled life which later resulted in her becoming a ward of the court. Jade fell in love with the art and used storytelling as a means of venting during her tumultuous times. Aging out of the system two years later, she was thrust into the dismal world of homelessness. Desperate, and with limited income, Jade began dancing full time at the tender age of eighteen.

It wasn't until Fall of 2008 when she finally caught her break after being accepted into Cleveland State University. There, Jade lived on campus and majored in Film and Television. Now, six years later, she flourishes from her childhood dream of becoming a bestselling author. Since then she has written the best-selling "Cameron" series.

Quite suitably, she uses her life's experiences to create captivating characters and story lines. Jade currently resides in Atlanta, Georgia. With no children, she spends her leisure shopping and traveling. She says that seeing new faces, meeting new people, and experiencing diverse cultures fuels her creativity. The stories are generated in her heart, the craft is practiced in her mind, and she expresses her passion through ink.

To learn more, visit www.jadedpublications.com

OTHER BOOKS BY JADED PUBLICATIONS!

JADED PUBLICATIONS Presents
Greek And Fiona
A Love Story
PEBBLES STARR
&
CHASE MOORE

CPSIA information can be obtained
at www.ICGtesting.com
Printed in the USA
LVOW12s1623130916
504435LV00002B/229/P